NATURE - CURE
FOR
HEALTH AND HAPPINESS

DIAMOND POCKET BOOKS PRESENTS

HEALTH SERIES

Title	Price
Brilliant Light (Reiki Grand Master Manual)	195.00
Unveiling the Secrets of Reiki	195.00
Natural Healing with Reiki	100.00
Health in Your Hands	95.00
Allopathic Guide for Common Disorder	125.00
Acupuncture & Acupressure Guide	95.00
Hair Care	60.00
Eye-Care	75.00
Be Your Own Doctor	60.00
Be Young and Healthy for 100 Years.	60.00
Surya Chikitsa	60.00
Ayurvedic Treatment for Common Diseases	95.00
Herbal/Treatment for Common Diseases	95.00
Add Inches	60.00
Shed Weight Add Life	60.00
A Complete Guide to Homeopathic Remedies	75.00
A Complete Guide to Biochemic Remedies	60.00
Common Diseases of Urinary System	75.00
Wonders of Magnetotherapy	75.00
Family Homeopathic Guide	75.00
Food For Good Health	95.00
Juice Therapy	60.00
Miracles of Urine Therapy	60.00
Causes and Cure of Stress	75.00
Diseases of Digestive System	75.00
Nature Cure for Health & Happiness	60.00
Family Homeopathic Guide	75.00
Causes & Cure of Diabetes	75.00
Ladies Slimming Course	60.00
Acupuncture Guide	50.00
Acupressure Guide	50.00
Yoga for Better Health	95.00
Joys of Parenthood	40.00
Diseases of Respiratory Tract	75.00
Ladies Health Guide	75.00
Skin Care	75.00
Common Diseases of Women	75.00
Complete Beautician Course	95.00
Beauty Guide	95.00
Sex for All	75.00
Pregnancy & Child Care	60.00
Tips on Sex	75.00
Vatsyanana Kamasutra	95.00
The Manual Sex & Tantra	40.00

ASTROLOGY, VASTU, PALMISTRY

Title	Price
Remedial Vaastushastra	200.00
Sampuran Vastu Shastra	200.00
Commercial Vaastu	200.00
Enviornmental Vaastu	150.00
Practical Vastushastra	150.00
Jyotish and Santan Yog	75.00
Wonder World of Jewels	150.00
Hindu, Traditions and Beliefs a Scientific Validity	150.00
Study of Omens	95.00
Comprehensive Vaastu	60.00
Wonders of Numbers	60.00
Hypnotism	95.00
Cheiro's Language of the Hand (Palmistry)	95.00
Cheiro's Book of Numerology	60.00
Cheiro's Astro Numerology & Your star	95.00
Cheiro's Book of Astrology	95.00

GENERAL BOOKS

Title	Price
Famous Tourist Centres of India	60.00
Pilgrimage Centre of India	95.00
India-A Travel Guide	300.00
Mathematical Puzzle	60.00
Selected Songs of Rafi (Roman)	50.00
Selected Songs of Kishore (Roman)	50.00
Selected Songs of Mukesh (Roman)	50.00
Selected Songs of Lata (Roman)	50.00
Laughing Jokes	50.00
Naughty Jokes	50.00
Society Jokes	50.00
Children Jokes	50.00
Delighting Jokes	50.00
Thrilling Jokes	50.00
Hilarious Jokes	50.00
7 Days to Power Memory (With Audio Cassette)	95.00
Dynamic Memory Methods	95.00
English : English-Hindi Dictionary	180.00
Rape of the Mountain : Kargil The Untold Story (With Picture)	95.00
3500 Names for Babies	60.00
Lovely Name for Male Child (4 Colour)	40.00
Lovely Name for Female Child (4 Colour)	40.00
Indian Microwave Cook Book	100.00
Non Vegitarian Cook Book	100.00
Vegitarian Cook Book	100.00
Beauty of Mehandi	20.00
Modern Design of Mehandi	30.00
The Making of Mahatma (A. Biography)	95.00
Messiah of Poor-Mother Teresa	40.00
Learn & Speak 15 Indian Languages	40.00
Diamond Essay and Letter Writing (For Senior Classes)	60.00

Order books by V.P.P. Postage Rs. 5/- per book extra. Postage free on order of three or more books, Send Rs. 20/- in advance.

Diamond Pocket Books (P) Ltd.
X-30, Okhla Industrial Area, Phase-II, New Delhi-110020, Phones : 6841033, 6822803, 6822804, Fax : (0091) -011-6925020

NATURE - CURE

FOR

HEALTH AND HAPPINESS

DR. SATISH GOEL

DIAMOND POCKET BOOKS

X-30, Okhla Industrial Area, Phase-2,
New Delhi-110020

ISBN 81-7182-024-7

© **Publisher**

Publisher	:	**Diamond Pocket Books Pvt. Ltd.,** X-30, Okhla Industrial Area, Phase-II, New Delhi-110020.
Phone	:	011-6841033, 6822803, 6822804
Fax	:	011-6925020
E-mail	:	mverma@nde.vsnl.net.in
Website	:	www.diamondpocketbooks.com
Edition	:	2001
Price	:	Rs. 95/-
Price US $	:	7/-

NATURE-CURE FOR HEALTH & HAPPINESS

Dr. Satish Goel   **Rs. 95/-**

PREFACE

"Nature never did betray the heart that loved her"—is what the doyen of the English Romantic poets, William Wordsworth, asserted cons ago but in our almost suicidal enthusiam to hit upon an artificial solutions to our natural problems, we are neglecting this vital truth. Was it not Gautam, the enlightened one, who also advised us that "Look unto yourself for solution to your problems?" The unbriddled growth of industrialism, accentuated by the haphazard and reckless development of modern science and technology has created a situation which prevents man from bestowing adequate care and attention even to his minimal personal health needs. Health is not something that can be purchased in a bottle from a drug store but a condition built over the years from within by our own vital process through conscientious efforts and self-control or will power. Good health is nature's gift to man, but man, being preoccupied with a mechanical life-style, has alienated himself from nature. It is to goad him to re-establish this rapport that this book has been devised. Included in it are mostly the therapies that are based upon the naturally available edibles. Let us eat our way to good health rather than hanker after the treatments which more damage our systems than cure their maladies. Also included is the yoga therapy which is an indispensible part of such treatments.

  Lastly the author wishes to convey his gratefulness to Mr. Narender Kumar, Managing Director of Diamond Pocket Books who provided him all help to devise this book.

Contents

I	Nature : The Source for Cure of all disorders	7
II	Principles of Naturopathy	13
III	The Basic Parameters Vital Force, Sleep, Diet, Sunlight, Clean Water	18
IV	Techniques And Methods Employed In this Therapy	31
V	The Juice Therapies 1. The Wheat-Grass Juice Therapy 2. Tulsi Therapy	37
VI	Fruit And Vegetable Therapies 1. Garlic Therapy 2. Amla (Emblic Myrohalans) Therapy 3. Lemon Therapy 4. Ginger Therapy 5. Papaya Therapy 6. Karela Therapy	74
VII	The Yoga Therapy, Human Body And The Cure of the Diseases	93
VIII	Your Food : Guidelines and Tables	122
IX	Traditional Naturopathic Treatment For Various Diseases	132
X	Summary Treatment Chart	151

CHAPTER I

NATURE: THE SOURCE FOR CURE OF ALL DISORDERS

Life is the manifestation of a judicious interactions between man and nature. It is only when man becomes indifferent to nature that he gets ill. Perpetual indifference to nature hastens one's termination as the vital being. Living as close to nature as possible has been an accepted way of keeping one fit. The more we start living in the unnatural surroundings, the greater are our chances of falling sick. In the modern urban life wherein living in a match box houses devoid of proper natural light and fresh air we find more and more persons falling sick than before. It is not an exaggeration to claim that now the span of youth is drastically getting reduced notwithstanding the marvels of the modern therapy system. It appears as if the greater the research in medical circles, the larger is the number of disease that appear to be plaguing our life.

Did we ever try to analyse that despite the decreasing mortality rate why we are having more old and sick in the society? We might now live for seventy years, about a few decades more than the earlier life span but without any youthful vigour and vitality. It is not uncommon to see the young lads of twenty and twenty-five not only losing their hair or having more grey hair but also finding their faces wrinkled with all sorts of advance age problems like high blood pressure, diabetes, spondylitis troubling them and sapping them of their vitality. So, are the so-called modern researches in the field of medicines enhancing the span of life or of death? Are we not having more sick and old in the population than healthy and youthful persons? Why is it that with all the better amenities of life we are not only losing our physical strength but the mental calibre also?

The answer to all these questions lies in our increasingly leaving contact with nature. Dwelling in our pigeon holes we have forgotten how to work in the sun, enjoy fresh air or listen to the chirp of birds and the hum of the bees. We have lost the taste of fresh vegetables in their tinned cousins, rejuvenating juices in their bottled versions which damage the body more than they claim to vitalise. Most of the time we seem to be passing an artificial life in artificial surroundings. We forget that our body is also part of nature and we can't sever its links with the root for long without suffering the deadly consequences. In fact most of the diseases are the bye product of the modern therapy itself. It must be understood at the very outset that the drug is not the way to good health but it is the way to further disease. Drugs usually cause relief for only a temporary duration from any disease. Constant consumption of drugs may develop side-effects or after-effects in the body. Supposed pain killers like Anacin, Aspirin, Novalgin, Crocin, Analgin, etc. may give temporary relief from pain but they will surely cause a permanent damage to the heart, liver and kidneys, leading to a much more deadly disease than they are supposedly curing. This defect is inherent in the allopathic therapy. As for other drug based system like Homeopathy or Biochemical therapies, they too are found inadequate in the modern stressful life. As a matter of fact no drug could be found fully reliable for longer duration without leaving some adverse effect. The whole trouble is our relying too much on drugs. Most of us become almost addict or the devotees of drugs. We generally believe that drugs affect the body. This belief is, however erroneous, the reality being quite contrary. It is in fact the body that acts upon the drugs and not vice-versa. No doubt this assertion may sound a little strange but it is true. In fact, not these drugs but there is a regulatory mechanism in the body that maintains its health. This is called 'Vital Force' or the 'Praana Shakti'. It is this vital force that combats diseases or any disorder of the body. This is a natural reaction—called reflex action—of the body. For example, if a particle of dust lodges in the eye, we experience a copious flow of water from the eye. This flow has one aim: to flush the particle out. Similar is the reaction of the body when any other disorder, or the foreign particle gets in. The vital force, till there is life in the body, tries to ensure that no unwanted foreigner intrudes its domain. The moment it comes, the whole body system automatically gets ready to fight it out. In fact, the job of an ideal medicine is to help the body to fight out the intruder quickly. This is not possible with any artificial drugs or chemical substances. It is only nature that provides best help to the body. That is the reason why most of the advance countries are increasingly accepting Naturo-therapy or Naturopathy as the safest and most effective therapy to keep the body fighting fit. They have realised the futility of the research in the field of drug based therapies.

A wide-ranging survey carried out in the United Kingdom in the seventh decade showed that nearly 90 per cent of the people had implicit faith in their family doctors, but within a span of nearly two decades the situation underwent such a drastic transformation that by the 90, they found that people reposing their faith in the doctors practising therapies based upon drugs was reduced to bare 30 pre cent only. This rapid erosion of faith is highly significant and suggestive.

It was not long ago that it appeared that man would win the battle against diseases and disorders finally and decisively with the help of the 'wonder drugs' that were being discovered at that time. New and improved equipment and method of diagnosis were being developed, and epidemics of infectious diseases were being brought under control one after the other. But when the people in the advanced countries found that even these medicines and wonder drugs were not the answer to their problem. They began to revert to the lap of mother nature for their good health. They argued to themselves that their forefathers were not fools who reposed so much faith in the natural products. They believed in what the modern, enlightened doctors are advising to their patients. Don't consume tablets but vegetables, no more you require mixtures and syrups with unpalatable taste but only juices and broths made from the natural product. This whole style of therapy—rather a discipline—is called food therapy. It has been invariably established that the use of improper food is perhaps the root cause of every disease. Raw food, vegetable and fruits are bitter for health than cooked or fried foods or food prepared in any other way. Compared to milk, juices of grapes, carrots, strawberries and raspberries are more effective for health and nourishment. Vegetables and fruits, their juices help to cure such disease as cannot be cured by modern-therapies, no matter how grandiloquent be the assertion of the celebrated so—called 'divine' medical journals.

Let us understand it that no disease can be wiped out merely by medication. What is necessary is that people should be inspired and encouraged to take an active interest in their own health, and to instruct them in the basic rules of preservation of health. This is the principal aim of naturopathy. Nature cure does not employ hit or miss methods so prevalent today. Naturopathy has a completely different attitude to the treatment of diseases Naturopathy defines disease as 'disease—an absence of the feeling of well-being generated by robust health'. Nature cure doesn't attempt to get rid of illness, but aims primarily at restorting health. It doesn't attempt a frontal attack on the diseases by endeavours to strengthen in natural defence of the body. In short, it is the body that affects the cure, not the physician.

It must be made clear at the very outset that although people are even increasingly turning to Nature Cure, many of them regard this system of therapy fundamentally in the same way as they regard other systems, and try to evaluate the curative methods of Naturopathy by the standards of other systems. A person suffering from a chronic disease goes to a Naturopath, and is told that it would be necessary to fast for two to four days, and that for the next few days only simple uncooked food would have to be taken. The response of such persons is invariably pleading against fast while citing the instructions of the doctors from other therapies. It is difficult to convince such patients that the task of freeing the body from the disease, and that of maintaining its strength and weight are different, and so the two cannot be accomplished simultaneously. If the patient keeps the precepts of the previous physicians in mind, and fasts, or restricts his diet, unwillingly, this uncooperative or positively negative attitude is bound to have an adverse effect on the body, resulting in weakness and slowing down of the rate of recovery. Hence it is absolutely necessary that the patient adopts a method of treatment in full faith and follows the prescribed regimen with utter sincerity.

Another important fact regarding this therapy is the prevalent confusion in the treatments based on Naturism and Naturopathy. It is for this reason not many people are able to distinguish between living in accordance with the laws of Nature (Naturism or Nature Worship) and the treatment of the disease based upon the laws of Nature or Naturopathy. The protagonist of Naturism exhort man to live in accordance with nature's laws. In their opinion, all the ills of mankind can be traced to one single cause—the artificial living of modern civilisation. Hence, in their opinion there is only one solution for its problems—Return to Nature. They advise us to reject all the appurtenances of civilisation right from fire to the Internet, and to live only on eating raw vegetables, fruits, bulbs but nothing of non-vegetarian category. Living in the open and leading a simple life have also been their favourite fads.

These Nature-worshippers had their considerable impact in Europe in the earlier part of this century. In Germany and Switzerland, the Nature worshippers went as far as to build Sanatoria where men and women of all ages led self-reliant lives, subsisting on vegetables and fruits, sleeping on the floor and living in the 'eternal communion with Nature' and going about all their affairs in the nude. The cult gained special popularity in Germany till the onset of Hitler's rule, who compelled these Nature worshippers to clothe themselves.

Against their style is pitted the ideology propounded by the proponents of Nature Cure or Naturopathy while the proponents of Naturism believe in returning to Nature, the believers of Nature Cure go even beyond Nature. The devotees of Naturism stop at worshipping Nature, but the adherents of Naturopathy endeavour to achieve a synthesis of such diverse but complementary elements as Nature and Art (human creation), past and future or in a nutshell, Nature and Civilisation. They do not believe that all the progress that civilisation has achieved over the millennia is valueless. However, they do recommend the rejection of those elements of civilisation which have not only proved damaging but positively devastating. Thus the proponent of nature concede the importance of Nature, but do not hesitate to assist nature in combating diseases and to hasten the restoration of health by the adoption of extraneous curative measures like water treatment (hydrotherapy), clay therapy, regimentation of the dietary, habits, magnetotherapy, acupressure, acupuncture etc. They wish to employ all natural methods to add to the efficacy of Nature and have the disease cured. That is precisely the reason why the expert Naturopaths do not consider diagnosis of disease superfluous. They do believe in carrying out various tests and investigations to ascertain the causes of the disease and other relevant facts before prescribing treatment, thus ensuring that the treatment is rational, sound and appropriate. They find deriving the advantages of the modern technological development quite logical. Besides, they also evaluate the progress of the process of recovering every few days. The treatment of common ailment is simple, but if there are some complications, variations and refinements in the treatment may become necessary. In the cases they find that the scope of treatment goes beyond the reach of nature cure they do not hesitate recommending alternate systems of medicine to the patient. For, like every good and moral practitioners believes, they also value the life and well-being of the patient more than their credit of curing him.

Of course, the naturopath wholeheartedly believes in leading completely natural life as an ideal but it appears that this ideal is not wholly achievable in the present era. Nevertheless it doesn't mean that they recommend a compromise with an artificial way of leading life. We must try to be as close to nature as possible but value of the life and well-being of the patient is still permanent and shall always be.

Having suffered all the trial and tribulations now the modern man also realises that answer to his all ills lies in the lap of nature. Man born in the lap of nature has now recognised the right direction of cultivating the delight of the body and the mind and of maintaining health by using natural food and juices. There is no doubt that mankind will find the source of real hope and joy in this new trend. It was not for nothing that the Father of Medicine, the ancient Greek thinker and physician advised to his countrymen, *"Let thy food be thy medicine!"*

CHAPTER II

PRINCIPLES OF NATUROPATHY

The first and foremost principle of Naturopathy is "*The principle of the unity of the causes of Disease.*" That is, the disease can't be treated in isolation. In this modern age of the specialisation people forget this basic principle. According to this principle there is one and only one cause of all the diseases and that is the accumulation of toxic and foreign substances in the body i.e. Toxaemia. It is when poisonous or foreign substances invade our body that we fall ill. There is no doubt that there are many contributory causes of such accumulation. As we all know, our body is made up of cells. Large numbers of these cells die which are replaced by new cells everyday. Now, the dead cells are foreign material to the body. In addition, some processes in the living cells also continuously form toxic wastes because of the metabolic reactions taking place in them. However, the prime cause of the accumulation of poisons is the artificiality of our ways of life. Improper, misguided and wrong ways of life cause the production of large amounts of toxic substances in the body. In case these poisons are not eliminated at a reasonably fast pace to counteract their production, our body is bound to get sick.So, to greater extent this style of living almost make us commit suicide.

These toxic wastes and poisons assert their presence in a variety of ways. The body may develop fever, swelling, pain and various other allied symptoms. As a matter of fact an acute disease is merely manifestation of the natural healing process in the body. No matter what names are given to the diseases there is only one root cause: toxic substances, presence in the body.

This theory is in direct variance to the modern medical sciences, theories which attribute cause of diseases to various bacterias, viruses, fungi and other micro-organisms. However, Naturopaths call this to be a totally erroneous belief. But, unfortunately, fed on this staple belief, the modern people are given to believe it to be true. It has been proved all over the world by the renowned naturopaths like Dr. Patinkoffer of the Vienna University, Dr. Powell of California—to name a few—that the germs do not cause the disease but only aggravate it. It has been found that 14,000 germs of TB, diphtheria, typhoid, cholera and other diseases enter the body of each of us every hour through water, food and the air we breathe in. Why then do we not all contract all these disease? It is obvious that if conditions in the body are not favourable for the growth and proliferation of the these bacteria, they are incapable of causing these diseases.

It has been established by various experiments that only twenty minutes are needed for the bacterium to grow and multiply. In eight hours the number of descendants of one bacterium rises to 16 million, and twenty-four hours to more than 5 billion. It means this number of bacteria should be sufficient to destroy the whole human race. This is just the progeny of a single bacterium! And we are fighting about 14,000 bacteria every hour! However, such phenomenal growth never actually occurs. For these bacteria if there is no food (poisons and wastes) they just cannot flourish in the body and eventually perish.

However, if they get enough of such wastes and poisons present in the body of any person, they begin to multiply rapidly. So if we do not provide them with their food, they can't survive.

So believing erroneously that these bacteria or germs etc. being the source of all ailments, the Allopathic School of Medicine developed a comparatively new style of treatment called antibiotic treatment. To try to destroy the germs by poisoning them with antibiotics, instead of attacking the root cause of disease, namely the accumulated poison in the body, is tantamount to making our body a battle ground for two different sets of toxic materials, which only result in harming the cells of the body and in the process weakening the Vital Force. It doesn't seem logical to risk grave side effects by consuming antibiotis to kill germs which are not responsible for creating that illness. The very name of the antibiotic treatment suggests that it is against life—as anti means against and bio means life! Without realising the purpose of this treatment we seem to be adopting it as a regular style of treatment. It began as the stop-gap arrangement. The whole edifice of this type of treatment rests upon the premises that by reducing the life-potency of the whole body, the ill-effect of the bacteria could also be reduced as they also derive nourishment from the body itself. This type of treatment is still in the experimental stage. That is why we see many medicines rejected every year although when they were produced they were held as the panacea. Hardly a hundred or a hundred and twenty-five years have passed since doctors polished off hundreds of patients by administering large doses of the highly poisonous substance known as CALOMEL. It was in the name of science that this terrible deed was done, and was not looked upon as a crime. But today it is condemned in the strongest terms. More recently penicillin has claimed not a few human lives. There are scores of such modern medicines which are heralded as the '*Modern Sanjeevani*',but in a few years are condemned as the '*Halaahal*' (deadliest poison)

Perhaps our discerning readers would like to ask if germs do not cause disease how does an epidemic spread so rapidly. And secondly, if germs really assist nature in eliminating toxic substances from the body, why do people die of disease? Also, why is the condition of the patient found to improve after the administration of antibiotics?

The answers, in the order of questions are given below in the explanation. First of all let us understand that it is purely an axiomatic belief that identical causes produce identical results. If we happen to observe the individuals making up our society with regard to their habits of eating and drinking, breathing, sleeping, dressing etc. and compare their residences and their sporting activities and life styles in general, it will be obvious that in all respects there is a very close resemblance. Now, if their life styles are so similar, would not all be equally weak and equally suscesptible in the same manner ? Would not the kinds and amounts of poisons in their bodies also be closely similar? Would not they suffer from diseases manifesting similar symptoms? This explanation accounts for the rapid increase of a disease during the spread of an epidemic. Conducive conditions make the germs swell at an alarming rate.

As for the second doubt, we are sure that there is no confusion regarding bacteria asserting Nature. The reason the patient does not get well is that we put impediments in the progress of the efforts instituted by the body to get rid of the disease with the help of bacteria. All the energies of the body should be enlisted in the fight against the diseases. Instead, despite the total absence of hunger, we keep feeding the patient, thus frittering away the energy of the body in efforts at digestion. Under such conditions even the eventuality of death cannot be ruled out although the author feels that life and death stay beyond the reach of any therapy. The therapies are effective only between them.

In the answer to the third doubt, our humble contention is that if the symptoms of a disease disappear, or the physical condition of the patient seems to be improving, after the administration of an antibiotic drug, it is only an illusion that the patient starts showing the symptom of improvement. The truth is that these medicines weaken the powers of resistance of the body to such an extent that the body drops its efforts (which we call the symptoms of the disease) to get rid of the disease. The acute disease, thus believed to have been suppressed, turns chronic. In short, it is the attenuation of the symptoms under the action of the medicines that we construe as an improvement in the health of the patient. Moreover, as the antibiotic drugs also contain some supportive analgesic or sedative drugs, the visual effect of the improvement of the patient condition is often due to his feeling less pain or restlessness. At times, suppressed by the antibiotic treatment the Vital Force is made to over work which though showing the improvement apparently, gets weakened permanently. That is the reason why in a growing body like those of the kids—even the seasoned allopaths refuse to administer antibiotic drugs. They know that a deficiency at this stage may have a serious repressions at a later stage.

In fact, the Naturopath deals the body as a one organic hole and hence the principle of the unity of causes of Disease. The second basic principle of Nature Cure is that it is nature that heals not the physician or the medicines. Before elaborating this point further we must understand the root of the term 'physis'. It is a Greek word and the root of all the words derived from it like the physician, physical etc. This root term stands for nature. Again, it is the physician whose main job is to strengthen nature. Unless and until the powers of resistance of the body are strengthened, it is just not possible to cure patients by use of medicines, or indeed by other methods. Giving an analogy it can be said that no good message can be received by only humouring the messenger. It is not he who 'creates' the message; he only delivers it. So the body could be strengthened only by making it capable to drive out the toxic material and retaining the vital ones. This is the very foundation on which the entire edifice of Naturopathy stands. That is precisely why all treatments in the Nature Cure System are directed to only one end: to strengthen the power of resistance—i.e. the Vital Force—of the body. The aiding tools to such treatment are various therapies called clay-therapy, hydrotherapy and massage, exercises, dietary regimen, sun-bathing etc. These shall be discussed one by one in the coming chapters. First of all, we wish to rivet the readers' attention to the basic parameters, which, according to Nature Cure are the symptoms to judge the health of a person.

CHAPTER III

THE BASIC PARAMETERS

The following parameters act as the barometers to judge the body's health.

A. **Vital Force** : The fundamental belief of naturopathy is the presence of the vital force in a human body. It is the vital force which keeps one alive and act as a protector against the onslaught of all diseases. It is a store house of one's physical strength, vigour, ebullience and one's nerve. The ebbing vital force results in a person having sickly face, a persistent headache and malfunctioning bowels. The *'Nature-Cure'* believes that *'Purush'* or a human body derives his strength from *'Prakrati'* or *'Nature'*. Hence naturopathy is very close to the Hindu belief which works on these fundamental parameters. Any imbalance between the forces active in a human body and the forces active in nature results in sickness and disease. To maintain this equilibrium of the said forces, one has to follow some simple rules with regard to sleep, rest, fresh air, sunlight and adhering to the norm of maintaining clean habits. Among these factors foremost important is sleep.

B. **Sleep** : It is supposed to be the best source to enhance and maintain your vital force. Sleep nourishes the body. No wonder Shakespeare had opined in one of his plays : *"Sleep ! The chief nourisher of the life's feast."* In fact sleep can be taken to be the barometer of one's health and vitality. When a child is born, his body is fresh and hence full of energy. And that is why a child sleeps for long hours. Immediately after the delivery, the child may sleep for 22 to 23 hours. Its growth in life results in the dimunition of sleep and as one approaches one's natural death, one is able to sleep hardly for couple of hours because the vital force starts ebbing from his body. It is more the sound sleep than a sumptuous meal that vitalises your whole body. Of course, both requirements of the body are interrelated but the fact is both are also dependent upon the other. It is only after our belly is full that we can have good sleep, conversely it is only that we have had a good sleep that we feel hungry. Sleep not only gives sure release from fatigue, but also replenishes the source of energy. The expenditure of energy during sleep is minimal. An old saying in Sanskrit asserts :*"Ardha-rog hare nidra sarva roga hare kshudha."*

C. **Diet** : Diet has a direct bearing upon one's state of health. This springs a question : Is there a relation between diet and health? What is the nature of this relationship? Each therapy has separately tried to answer this question which vary from their total perception of the human body vis-a-vis their ailment.

Although allopathy seems to be ruling the roost in the so-called modern world, its attitude towards diet is rather casual. It advises a 'balanced' diet i.e. diet that contains the requisite proportions of proteins, carbohydrates, fats, vitamins and minerals. But most of the doctors are not much concerned about their patient's diet. Their standard advice is *"Eat whatever you like but only in moderate quantities."* This is a very evasive advice. The old school of Indian medicine, the Ayurveda has gone a little deeper into this question of the inter-relationship of diet and health. It classifies all foods into categories like phlegm—promoting or phlegm—destroying, bile-promoting and bile-destroying and the like. It also differentiates among the various edibles as being 'heavy' or 'light' on the system. However because of lack of further research in the field their answer to this question in not very clear.

In Nature-cure-therapy diet is that bedrock upon which the whole edifice stands. In this system, a detailed study has been made of the merits and demerits of each food and drink. Proper diet can be a veritable elixir of life, lifting one to the pinnacle of health, improper diet, on the other hand, can act as a poison, destroying health and life.

First of all, it must be understood as to what is the purpose of food intake. It serves basically two functions: supplying essential nutrient to the body, and maintaining acid-alkali balance in the blood. Let us consider the first purpose of food.

ESSENTIAL ITEMS OF FOOD

The five ingredients of food essential for the nutrition of the body are : proteins, carbohydrates, fats, vitamins and minerals.

(i) **Proteins** : Proteins are essential for the growth, maintenance and regeneration of the body. The main sources of proteins are pulses, milk, eggs, meat etc. All proteins are made up of amino acids and different proteins contain different proportion of the various amino acids. There are in all twenty three amino acids in food proteins. Out of these there are ten that the human body cannot synthesise: Arginine, Histidine, Isolencine, Leucine, Lysine, Methionine, Phenylamaine, Theonine, Truptophane and Valine. These are called 'essential' amino acids. The body must be supplied with requisite amounts of these amino acids through food. The rest of the amino acids can be synthesised by the body from these. Their sources are the following :

Arginine : Alfalfa, green leafy vegetables, carrots, beetroots, cucumber, celery, lettuce, radishes, potatoes. These are essential for the maintenance of muscles, cartilage cells, reproductive organs, prevention of sterility.

Histidine : Radish, carrot, beetroot, celery, cucumber, garlic, onion, turnip, alfalfa, spinach, apple, pineapple, pomegranate, papaya. It is needed for liver, haemoglobin and semen.

Isolencine : Papaya, olives, coconut, almond, apricot, pistachios, walnut. It is needed for thymus, spleen, pituitary gland, haemoglobin, regulation of metabolism.

Leucine : All the foods listed in the above category. It is needed for counter balancing isolencine.

Lysine : Carrot, beetroot, cucumber, celery, mint, spinach, turnips, alfalfa, germinated soyabeans, papaya, apple, plum.

Methionine : Cabbage, cauliflower, garlic, pineapple, apple. It is needed for maintaining haemoglobin, spleen and pancreas.

Phenylalanine :Carrots, beetroots, spinach mint, tomatoes, pineapples, apples. It is needed for elimination of foreign substances, kidneys, urinary bladder.

Thereonine : Carrots, alfalfa, green leafy vegetables, papaya. It is needed to make good the deficiency of some other amino acids.

Truptophane : Carrot, beetroot, celery, spinach, alfalfa, turnip. It is needed for regeneration of cells, secretion of digestive juices, eyes.

Valine : Carrot, turnip, sweet gourd, celery, mint, beetroots, tomato, apple, pomegranate, almonds. It is needed for essentially a female body because it keeps the breasts and ovaries in good health.

Rest of the 13 amino acids could be generated by the body with its interaction from these amino acids. Many nutritionist believe that animal proteins are superior and indeed complete while vegetable proteins are inferior, incomplete and second class protein. This belief, however, is erroneous. By combining vegetable proteins in proper proportions we can get all the essential amino acids in the requisite amounts. In fact, ingestion of excessive amounts of proteins results in the formation of uric acids, which is harmful to health. Many of the diseases troubling mankind have their roots in the excessive intake of proteins.

(ii) **Carbohydrates**: Carbohydrates provide heat and energy to the body. Cereals, tubers, roots, pulses, milk etc. are the main sources of carbohydrates. There can be no objection to the use of natural carbohydrates in their original forms. But the use of processed carbohydrates is not desirable. De-branned flour, polished rice, white flour, refined sugar etc. are instances of such processed foods. Processing removes the fibres and roughage from food. This results in insufficient elimination of wastes. Toxic substances, consequently, accumulate in the blood. We cause a lot of damage to our health by consuming canned and bottled fruits, fruit juices, tomato ketchup, jams, jellies, instant Gulab-jamuns, ready ground flours, cakes, chocolates, and similar other processed carbohydrates. As such foods are easily over eaten, the digestive organs and subjected to understandably heavy loads. The consequence is severe indigestion and obesity, resulting later in more or less permanent diseased conditions like diabetes or disorders of the joints.

(iii) **Fat** : Like carbohydrates, fats, too perform the function of supplying heat and energy to the body. Ghee (classified butter) and Oils are the main sources of fats for vegetarians.

Fasts are basically of two types : saturated and unsaturated. Prolonged use of saturated fats causes constriction and hardening of the arteries, which may result in hypertension, heart attack and other related ailments. It is, therefore, necessary to minimise the intake of saturated fats, replacing them, if at all necessary by unsaturated fats.

Foods containing saturated fats are : butter, ghee, vegetable ghee, coconut oil, palm oil, whole milk, cream, khoya-based preparations, sweets prepared in ghee and vegetable ghee, whole-milk preparations (shreekhanda, basaundhi, ice-cream, pedas etc..), chocolates, cakes, biscuits, wafers, eggs, fat, meat, oysters, fish.

Foods containing unsaturated fats are : Peanut oil, seasame oil, maize oil, soyabean oil, cottonseed oil, sunflower oil and dishes prepared from these oils.

(iv) **Vitamins and Minerals** : Although the body needs only minute quantities of these substances they are of great importance. They perform various important functions in the body. Vitamins are essential for the proper digestion and absorption of proteins, carbohydrates and fats, and the development of the ability of the body to protect itself against diseases. Various minerals are needed for the formation and functioning of the cells. These vital substances are necessary for the maintenance of health. They are all the more necessary in sickness. Various disorders are the direct results of the deficiency of vitamins and minerals.

During an illness, the stores of vitamins in the body get quickly depleted. Improper diet, mental distress, pollution, smoking and addiction to drugs are other factors that destroy the vitamins in the body. In an estimate made by the doctors it was found that smoking of one cigarette destroys about 25 gms of vitamin C. Other vitamins are also destroyed in analogous ways. On the other hand the requirements of vitamins have increased manifold these days due to the mental stresses and worries which have becomes so common in modern times.

It is quite clear from the above analysis that man needs vitamins and minerals today as never before. Adequate quantities of these essential components of foods are available in uncooked foods, germinated grains and beans as well as in fruits, vegetables and their juices. It is high time we realised that cooking destroys vitamins. The vitamins in fruits and vegetables are rapidly lost if they are not immediately consumed after peeling or cutting them.

Some dieticians claim that vitamin B_{12} can be obtained only from meat. But they forget that we are civilised now and that meat is not eaten raw. And the moment it is cooked most of the vitamin B_{12} gets destroyed.

The vitamins in natural foodstuffs are in a 'live' and easily digestible form, and so are quickly and completely assimilated in the body. On the other hand, experiments have decisively proved that the expected benefit is almost never afforded by the use of the synthetic vitamins in the forms of tablets, pills etc. In the same way the body can't satisfactorily utilise artificially synthesised or purified mineral salts. In short if the body lacks minerals, the deficiency cannot be made good by medicines.

(v) **Acid and alkali balance in blood**: Normally the acid-alkali ratio in blood is generally 20:80. Maintenance of this ratio is essential for keeping good health. In fact healthy body naturally asserts itself to maintain this balance.

The foods also leave their alkaline-acidic residual effect after undergoing the fully cycle of digestive and metabolic processes. We may classify foods as alkali-genic and acid-genic respectively. Generally the acids produced by the metabolic activities (such as uric acid, lactic acid etc.) which react with the alkalis in the blood, lymph, bile etc. thus being neutralised and rendered innocuous. But if our diet is replete with acid-genic food, the body cannot cope with all the resulting acids when the acids accumulate in the blood, symptoms associated with acidic blood like fatigue, headache, anorexia, insomnia, nervous tension, hyper-acidity, coryza etc. begin to appear.

In fact, acidic blood is an abnormal condition that hinders the physical development of children and adolescents, causes degeneration in older people and diminishes vitality. It causes difficulties in pregnancy and lactation. It is the origin of diseases like measles, appendicitis, pneumonia, tuberculosis and even cancer. It is clear from this analysis that all the toxic substances in the body are in the form of acids, and that in order to prevent or counteract the accumulation of acids in the body we must take food that is mainly alkali-genic. The table below shows which foods leave what effect on the system.

Alkali-Genic Foods		Acid-Genic Foods	
Foods	Alkali-Genic effect in %	Foods	Acid-Genic effect in %
Fruits		**Cereals**	
Fish (fresh)	27.81	rice (polished)	17.96
Raisins	15.10	rice (manually de-husked)	3.86
Grapes	7.15	cake	12.31
Sugar-cane	14.57	bread	10.99
Tomatoes	13.67	barley	10.58
Lemons	9.90	white flour (wheat)	8.32
Oranges	9.61	maize	5.37
Plums	5.80	wheat	2.66
Dates	5.50		

Alkali-Genic Foods		Acid-Genic Foods	
Foods	Alkali-Genic effect in %	Foods	Acid-Genic effect in %
		Pulses & Legumes	
Peaches	5.40	All pulses and	
Apricots (fresh)	4.79	legumes are acid-	
Bananas	4.38	genic	
Pomegranates	4.15	**Nuts**	
		peanuts	16.39
		walnuts	9.22
Coconuts	4.09	almonds	2.19
Pineapples	3.59	Food of animal origin	
Peas	3.26	(excluding milk)	
Watermelons	1.83	yolk of egg	51.83
Apples	1.38	White of Egg	8.27
		Eggs	11.61
Vegetables, Tubes & Roots		beef	38.61
Spinach	28.01	Chicken	24.32
Suva Plants	18.36	Goat' Flesh	20.30
Leafy Salad Plants	14.12	Fish	19.52
Cucumbers	13.50	Pork	12.47
Beetroots	11.37	**Milk Products**	
Turnips	10.80		
Sweet Potatoes (Yama)	10.31	Cheese	17.49
Radishes	6.05	Butter	4.33
Potatoes	5.90		
Peas (fresh)	5.15		
Cabbage	4.02		
Cauliflower	3.04		
Onions	1.09		
Pumpkins	.28		
Milk & Milk Products			
Skimmed Milk	4.89		
Cream	2.66		
Human Milk	2.25		
Cow's Milk	1.69		
Butter Milk	1.31		
Goat's Milk	.25		

Note : See more charts given in the last but one chapter.

It is, however, quite possible to maintain a balance between the acids and alkalis in the body by a judicious combination of various unprocessed cereals, raw vegetables, fruits and nuts in our daily diet and thus keep diseases at bay. Not only do the alkalis in such foods neutralise the acids in other foods, but they also help in extracting the acids and toxins accumulated in the cells of the body and in ejecting them from the system. These qualities make a diet made up of Alkali - genic components not only pure and wholesome, but also an efficient eliminating and cleansing agency.

We must realise that food is a necessity for the body, not for tongue. Meals planned with only the titillation of the taste buds as the principal aim are scarcely suitable for the nutrition of the body. Cooking the food for longer duration and adding spices would no doubt make it very tasty but in effect nutritionless. Cooking not only destroys vitamins and enzymes in the food, but also results in degsadation of their nutritive value. Proteins in food are evacuated and hardened by cooking. Such coagulated proteins are not digested but they decay in the digestive track. Cooking also makes carbohydrates less easy to digest. As a result they are not absorbed completely in the intestines. Thus in terms of nutrients our cooked food are almost valueless. A healthy person may still be able to extract the residual nutrients from them, but this is hardly possible for one who is ailing and whose need for them, therefore, is definitely more.

Shed off your notion that raw food is indigestible, and will cause heaviness in the belly or ache and gas in the stomach. It has been established by experiments that cooked foods require five to six hours for complete digestion, while raw food need only three to four hours. Fruit and vegetable juices are digested, and begin to get alsorbed in only 25 to 30 minutes. Thus uncooked food, and especially uncooked liquid food, affords rest for the digestive organs. The valuable energy of the body is not wasted in useless, futile attempts at digesting the indigestible and thus becomes available for regeneration and healing

COMBINATION OF FOODS FOR EASY DIGESTION

Proper digestion becomes easy if the combination of foods is right. If these rules are violated, even good nutritious food may produce toxic material as a result of decomposition in the digestive tract. For instance, there is no enzyme in the stomach which can digest carbohydrates. These are digested either in the mouth or in the small instentines on the other hand, the digestion of proteins takes place in the stomach. Let us consider a meal that contains large quantities of both carbohydrates and proteins. If it is masticated properly, the enzymes in the saliva in the mouth carry out partial digestion of the carbohydrates. But if the food is swallowed without proper mastication, the carbohydrates will remain undigested in the stomach while the proteins would get digested. They will therefore decay and produce toxic materials. In case of the chapatis (cooked loaf of flat bread), if a morsel of chapatis is chewed well the carbohydrates in it will be converted into sugars, imparting a sweet taste to the morsel. These sugars are directly absorbed into the blood stream as soon as they reach the stomach. Now if the chapatis are not chewed properly, the carbohydrates remain in a completely undigested form. With the result they start decaying in the stomach. An important point to be noted is that the enzymes in the saliva can act only in an alkaline medium. If sour chutneys or pickles are taken along with a morsel of the chapati, on if the vegetable on dal taken with chapati contains limes, tomatoes, tamarind or similar sources of acids, the enzyme in the saliva get de-activated and therefore completely undigested carbohydrates find their way into the stomach. Hence it is advisable not to have too many sour foods with chapatis for their mixture is conducive to creating toxic substances in the body.

The above analysis forms a combination sets for ideal consumptions. Observe the following rule and keep fit :

(X) Sour foods and carbohydrates go ill together. Hence they ought to be eaten separately.

(Y) Large amounts of proteins and large amounts of carbohydrates should not be taken in the same meal.

(Z) Large amount of proteins should not be taken simultaneously with large amounts of fats (e.g. dal and ghee). In certain cases it is permissible like ghee with Urad Dal. Moreover, proteins foods should not be ingested with sour fruits. For instance if lemon juice or tomatoes are added to dal, the acids in these fruits cause a dimunition in the secretion of digestive juices, rendering digestion less efficient. Look below the chart to have right combination for food intake.

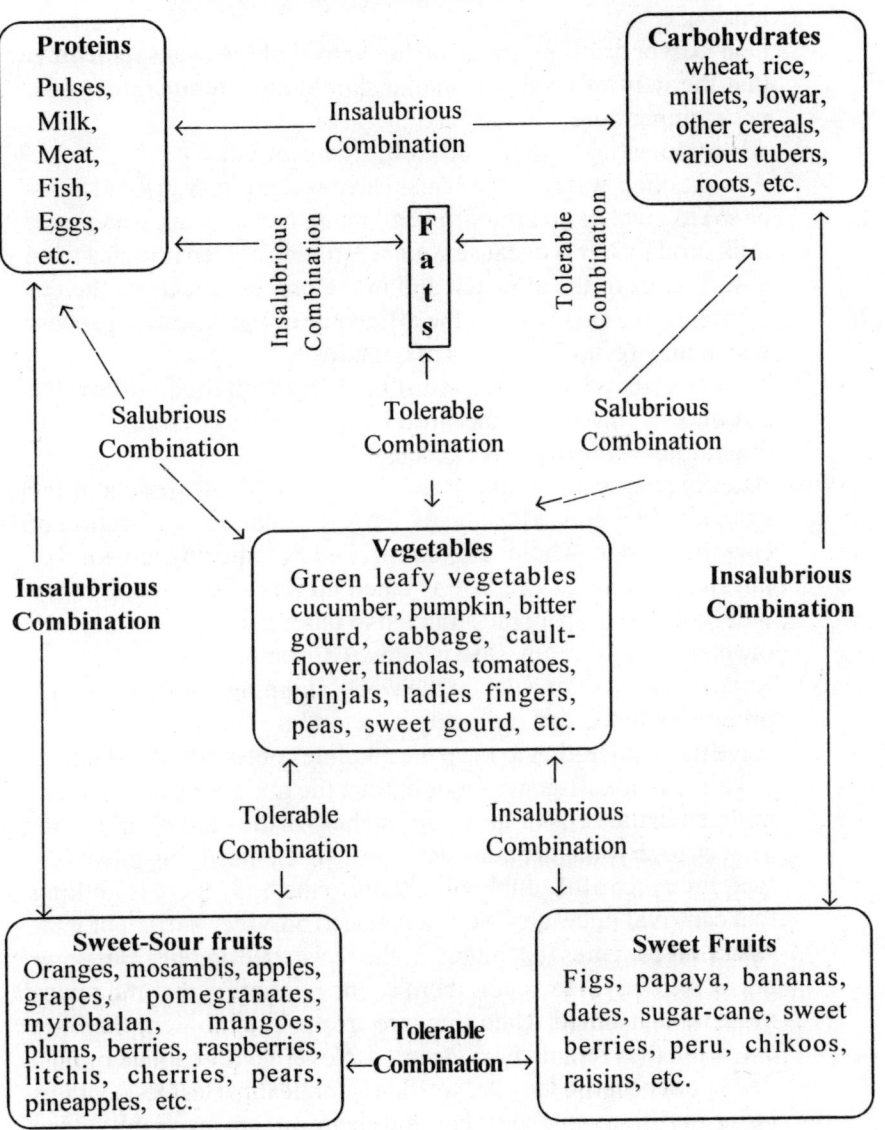

Some salient points for maintaining good health
(i) Always have foods in the right combinations
(ii) Don't eat when you don't feel hungry.
(iii) Don't eat when you are under some kind of physical or mental tension.
(iv) Don't eat or drink anything too hot or too cold. Always remember that the item of food you intake should have temperature near your temperature.
(v) Always masticate your food well, whatever you eat.
(vi) Avoid taking water with meals. Have water either prior (15 mts or so) to meal or an hour after full meal. Never drink water over milk products. It is because water requires only ten minutes to be absorbed from the stomach and in the process it carries the enzymes away. This reduces the efficiency of the digestive process which may result in the loss of appetite.
(vii) Never overeat. Never over-stuff the belly with food. Follow the old maxim that leave one-third stomach always empty for the operations of the digestive process.
(viii) After meals, rest a while. It is because the blood vessels of the stomach dilate just after meals. This stimulates the secretion of enzymes and thus helps digestion. If work requiring any kind of physical or mental exertion is taken up just after a meal, blood will be diverted from the stomach to other parts of the body like the hand, feet or brain, slowing down digestion.
(ix) Keep fast at least one day in the week, skipping one cereal meal, preferably lunch and replacing it by total fruit meal.
(x) Have more juice-diet to keep the alkaline content of blood intact. Alkaline or alkali-genic foods extract the toxic substances accumulated in the cells of the body and help in the their elimination. That is, such foods are considered to be body-purifying agents. In fact, for a plentiful supply of Alkalis to the body there is nothing that can rival juice-diet. Such a diet also provides sufficient vitamins and enzymes that augment the resistance and healing powers of the body. However, there is one restriction that the juices must be consumed when they are fresh. The moment they are extracted they should be consumed. Never go for canned or bottled juices because they are worthless for health. Besides containing no nutritive value some harmful chemicals are invariably added as preservatives. Besides the fact that must of the so-called fresh juice are synthetic, they are in fact harmful to the consumer. The

variety of inexplicable ailments that seemed to be plaguing the western countries are mainly due to the westerners depending more upon the canned stuffs.

Fasting : Apart from the juice-diet regimen one should also learn how to keep fast. Fasting doesn't only mean not having solid or cereal food but it has its full regimen. In Sanskrit or Hindi there are two terms whose loose English translation is 'fasting.' These terms are *'Vrat'* and *Upvaas'*. Literally they mean 'a determination' and *'living in an alternative way'* respectively. The inherent meaning in the modern parlance is shunning the food. So fasting means not only shunning the food but following a separate regimen that particular day. Begin your day with luke-warm lime-water and after morning rituals and bath, have only fruits. Have juices at about 11 a.m. or so and then juices or butter milk or curds in the afternoon. If you are habitual, have a cup of tea with fresh potato wafers or any other light salt-snacks you like. Keep on having plenty of water in between your this frugal diet. Then have light meal of chapatis, pulses, boiled vegetables, plentiful of salad etc. at your dinner and complete the ritual with milk before you retire for the day. Following this pattern, mutatis mutandis your special preference with the given range of choice, at least once in a week would not only keep your body clear of the toxins but also in good health, with all its organs functioning to the best of their efficiency.

D. **Sun-Light** : After proper sleep and adequate diet, what you need is the sun-light. The absence of the sun-light whithers a plant and this deficiency effects the human body in equal measure. The sun is the source of light and energy to nature, so naturally it also nourishes a human body and makes it strong. Your body gets Vitamin D from the sun-light, though not directly. If your body has enough of Vitamin 'A', the body's proper exposure to sun converts it into Vitamin 'D'. Especially in the winters we long to bask in the sun more because our body's requirement of Vitamin 'D' enhances. However in a tropical country like India, one should be worry of bathing in the sun-light with proper protection. One should never face the sun directly. In is an old saying in India that let your back get the maximum sun-light while the warmth of fire should be taken direct on the face. Moreover, owing to the dissipation of the ozone layer there is every chance of some harmful radiation also coming with the sun-light. So avoid sun-light direct on to your face but have it plentiful on your back. Proper exposure to the sun-light also strengthens the body. Try to accept sunlight on your body in every season to the bearable limits. In summers or rainy seasons have a little exposure of the sun-light on your body either at the day-break or at the sun-set time.

E. **Clean-Water** : Notwithstanding it being an essential requirement of the body, it is increasingly becoming precious, particularly in the metropolitan cities. One must ensure its supply in the purest form. Water is the cheapest and best cleansing agent. Drink it as much as you can but not with food. Because, if taken during the meals water disturbs the digestive process of the body. Read more about its importance in the 'diet-section' of this look. Water is also essential to cleans your body or bathe it in Naturopathy recommends only cold bath.

In short, the basic parameters to judge the body's essential requirement, according to Nature-Cure, is what the term 'Nature-Cure' suggests. Live as close to nature as possible. Eat chiefly those foods that are available in their natural form. It recommends proximity with Nature and what Hippocrates said : *"For the sick the least is the best"*

CHAPTER IV

TECHNIQUES AND METHODS EMPLOYED IN THIS THERAPY

(I) TAKING AN ENEMA

If you are on a diet of fruits or fasting, it is essential that your bowels must remain clean. For that taking an enema is a must. The water for the enema should be lukewarm and quantity about 1 to 1½ litres. For taking an enema take the following precautions :

(a) Always use the hard surface as your base for taking the enema. You can do so while lying on the floor but make sure your buttocks remain a few inches higher than the floor. Only then the introduction of the liquid to your body through the rectum can be done properly.

(b) Keep the vessel having lukewarm water hanging from a nail at least three feet higher than your body level. Insert the nozzle through the rectum and raise your knees a bit to facilitate the passage of water to your rectum.

(c) Check the apparatus before you actually use it. Clean the nozzle thoroughly and disinfect it properly before using it. Allow a little of water to pass through the nozzle before you start using it. This way no air packet will disturb the water's flow. The trapped air can penetrate the intestine with the enema water.

(d) When the water is inside the rectum, retain it for a couple of minutes before you go to the toilet. While inside the toilet, do not exert pressure to pass stool. If you wish your intestines to be also cleaned, use about 2.5 litres of cold water. You can use this enema daily without the apprehension of any harm. Cold water would help toning up the intestine muscles. Never put pressure on your system while passing out the enema water. Let it come out automatically with the filth. Initially you might take longer time in the toilet but soon your system will acclimatise itself to enema water and you'd pass out enema water and stool in normal time.

(II) USING MUD PACKS

A mud pack is made by taking the soft soil and adding water to it to make a soft dough like mud pack. The pack should stick and not be thin enough to flow out. Normally, a mud pack is applied on the abdomen, between the navel and the pubes area. It is better if you spread the mud evenly on a piece of cloth and the pack about half an inch thick. When you have placed the pack, remove the cloth and place a thick woollen cloth over it to cover the pack. Use the pack for about 20 to 30 minutes. When you remove the pack, clean the skin covered by the pack with a soft muslin cloth dipped in cold water. In case you find the soil of the pack is of sticking nature, add some sand to it before making the pack. Then it could be removed easily.

(III) HIP BATH

Take a special tub having one end rather raised up. Place yourself in it in such a way that your head is resting against the raised end and feet hanging out and resting on a stool. The level of water is such as to touch your navel while you sit in the tub. Your posture of sitting should be half-reclining. While sitting in the tub, rub your abdomen with a rough towel, right to left. Don't rub your skin too harshly and do not exert any pressure while doing so. The duration of hip bath can very from 10 to 20 mts., depending upon the basic body structure of the patient. The person with thin body may take hip bath for 10 mts. and the stout ones for 20 minutes. In winters the duration should be further reduced from 4 to 2 mts. When you start taking the hip bath, do it so for just a minute or two and then gradually increase the duration. If you feel the day temperature to be too low, rub your body vigorously for 5 to 7 mts. before taking the bath. This vigorous rubbing would heat up your body and you would not be discomfited due to the coldness of the season. Wash your body vigorously with a rough towel and dress quickly. Then after the sturdy ones may take up any other exercise or start jogging while the weak ones must wrap themselves in a warm blanket and rest for half an hour. Only then their body would be sufficiently warmed up. Have your normal bath a few hours after your hip bath but not before. When you start taking it regularly, you would know the correct technique of taking the hip bath.

(IV) BATHING THE GENITAL ORGANS

The essential part of this bath is to make your bottom and genital portion partially immersed in water. You can place a stool about a foot long, six inches wide and six inches high, having a circular cut in the front. If such a stool is not available, you can keep four bricks, two upon two, to raise the level and sit on them. The water level should be just an inch above the stool. The water should be cold. When you have made the apparatus ready sit over it and gently rub your abdomen with a piece of cloth dipped in the water. Do so for two minutes or so. Then the men should hold the foreskin of their penis by two fingers and rub it lightly with a soft piece of cloth for about 10 to 20 mts., depending upon your body structure. The ladies should also rub their abdomen and having pulled apart the lips of their vagina, rub them softly with a piece of soft cloth. The ladies should take these bath after their menstruation. Having rubbed the foreskin, rub the entire spine with a wet towel for two minutes. After finishing your genital bath, you can do your regular physical exercise to warm up you body. If your are too weak to do so, wrap your body in a warm blanket to restore warmth to your body.

(V) HOT BATH OF THE FEET

Take a bucket full of hot water and immerse your legs upto knees in it. Make sure that the water is not too hot to scald your feet or just lukewarm to turn cold very soon. When this water turns cold, go on adding hot water to it. While immersing your feet in the hot water, keep your body covered with a blanket. No harm if the blanket covers your bucket too! But all this while, keep your head covered with a towel soaked in cold water. Go on sipping hot water during this session of your feet bath. Take this hot bath for about 20 mts. Then wash your feet with cold water and wipe them dry with a rough towel. You can have your normal bath after you have had your hot-feet-bath.

(VI) NORMAL BATH

Bathing daily is more a ritual than a ceremony. Unfortunately, most of the people are not aware of its importance in keeping a body healthy. Besides being a process through which we clean our body, it is an ideal exercise to enhance the circulation of blood in our body and provide a much needed mild exercise to the limbs.

One should take bath daily in such a way that each limb of the body is cleaned. Just standing beneath the shower won't do! One should rub his body vigorously with the help of a soap or a piece of lemon or other cleansing agent. The bath should have two basic purposes: the cleanliness of the body and enhancing the blood circulation. It is better to clean the body treating each limb as a separate department. Begin from the feet and gradually move towards the head. Then rub your body dry with help of a rough towel. This will help the clogged pores due to dirt and sweat. The skin of the body has millions of pores through which the skin breathes, exactly like we breathe through the lungs. Although the cold bath is the best method to freshen your body, those who regularly take bath twice daily would do well to have hot bath at least twice a week when they retire for the day. A bath, hot or cold, should be taken one hour before meals or three hours after it. A hot bath would bring a sense of lethargy which will help in inducing sleep earlier. But make sure you do not stand in a very cool place the moment you step out of a hot shower. Sudden change of temperature is very bad for health. In case you are suffering from cold, take a hot bath and lie on your bed covering yourself with the quilt or blanket. This bath will drive out cold from your body. In winters, if your take a cold bath, try to dry up your body by rubbing it with your palm. It would be doubly beneficial to you. Besides getting a pleasant sensation, your skin would glow with pink health.

(VII) SUN-BATH

In naturopathy sun-bath is of vital importance. Unlike the Western style where sun-bath has more cosmetic than therapeutic value, in Indian condition it is ideal to take bath between 6 a.m. and 6-30 a.m. in the summers and 7 to 7.30 a.m. during the winters. You just take off all your clothes in a secluded place and let your body soak the effect of sunlight. In case you can't find a secluded place then you can take sun-bath covering your body with a fine muslin cloth. At times people sweat more. But don't wipe that sweat after a sun-bath. Let it dry normally. Some people have their pores clogged in. For them also sun-bath is ideal to activate their sweat glands. Some people might not perspire in the beginning but they would do so after three four days. You can also go on sipping hot water while taking sun-bath to induce sweating from the inside heat also.

(VIII) SPONGING

In case you are down with fever, it is better if you do regular sponging of the body. Cover your body with a blanket or a sheet and ask your intimate friend or relation to sponge your body with a wet towel, beginning from feet. Then rub the whole body with a dry towel for three to four minutes—your all the major body-limbs. Divide time equitably to get sponging finished in half an hour or so. The ideal time for sponging the patient is mid-day.

(IX) FASTING

Fasting is one of the most potent factor in Naturopathic cure. The main purpose of the fasting is to cleanse the body of all the refuse, hence poison. When you do fasting for a day, have only water throughout the first day. The normal intake of water should be around 2.5 litres of clean water with a few drops of lemon put in if your system is not prone to having acidity. Then, on the second day, have a very frugal diet of very light soup and boiled (easily digestible) vegetables like green long pumpkin ('Ghiya' or 'Lauki'). You can supplement it by light fruits. The idea is to make sure that your cleansed system is not immediately loaded with heavy food. Next day have only frugal diet of bread and moong-dal. Only from the third day of the fast you can have your normal food.

The period of fast depends on many factors: the problem, your own age, weight and the like.

(X) YOUR FOOD

The best quality of food for human system, according to naturopathy is that which is least treated by artificial means. That is why the best wheat flour is prepared by grinding wheat through a hand mill (chakki). While doing so, do not pass flour through a sieve so that the bran is not separated. Bran is the substance which provides roughage needed to avoid constipation. Moreover it contains the necessary vitamins. Knead the dough twice or thrice before making chapatis.

Porridge is another dish which is favourite of the naturopaths. Good quality, properly cleaned wheat should be used for being ground into porridge. Each wheat grain should be broken into eight to ten pieces. Flour and larger pieces should be separated and the porridge be roasted over a hot plate lightly till it turns brown. Then cook it like rice is cooked over a slow fire till properly done. Eat it as it is, without adding salt or sweet-milk. If you wish to sweeten it, add a few raisins to it.

Similarly, unmilled rice is ideal for the system. The milled rice has most of its necessary vitamins shed off during the process of milling and polishing. Add only as much water to rice as is absolutely necessary to make it retain the vital elements in it.

Eat vegetables with their rind on. Eat them unpeeled. If the rind of any vegetable is really hard, scrap it with a sharp knife. Wash the vegetables thoroughly before cutting them into small pieces. Try to eat vegetables in their raw form. If you want to cook certain vegetables, do so in a very little oil or ghee with only cuminseeds and salt thrown in for making the taste. Cook it on very slow fire to retain their vitamins and minerals, etc. Most of the vegetables contain natural water so you need not add extra water while preparing it. A dash of turmeric may also be added to the cooked vegetables. In case you wish some ghee to be added to it, do so when the vegetable is off the fire.

Raw vegetables and fruits can also be eaten in salad form. All the vegetables which can be eaten raw can form a part of salad. The main constituents of salad are: cucumber, carrots, raddish, onions, tomatoes, spinach, green coriander leaves, beet-root and cabbage. A normal adult must consume at least 250 gms. of salad per day. You may add lemon-juice and a little of salt in your salad to make it more tasty and palatable. Alternatively, you can have fruit salad also, before the meal.

The interval between two meals ought to be minimum five hours or more. Have your last meal at least three hours before you retire for the day and go to sleep. The ideal meal times for the day ought to be: breakfast at 7 a.m., lunch at 12 noon, fruit juices or fruits at 4 p.m. and dinner at 7 p.m. In between the meals, drink as much water as possible. One should drink at least 2.50 litres of water in a day. Water not only helps in maintaining the ideal body-temperature, it helps in clearing the toxic elements in the body. However, if you can't stop taking water during the meals, have it very little—especially in summers—mainly to wash down the food with it.

Always chew your food as much as possible before swallowing it. Unchewed or underchewed food creates the problem and your intestines will have to exert more. An ancient belief of the old physician of India—to chew food at least 32 times, one chewing for each tooth—is very correct. If you chew food well, you'd be automatically requiring much less water to wash your food down.

CHAPTER V

THE JUICE THERAPIES

Haven't you heard of the Gods whose staple juice diet was only Somras? There is no reference of their taking any cooked or uncooked food except this potion which is supposed to be elixir to their life. When we remove the slough of myth we learn one basic fact that some herbs had that not only life sustaining but even life reviving quality. This is precisely the reason why the consumption of the raw juices shows a miraculous results where even medicines and injections fail to cure a disease.

In fact, fruit-juices (which are mainly drunk raw) are more effective than medicines on the kidney. That is why this entire therapy is more effective on the ailments of liver, kidney, to some extent skin. There are some special juices like 'Cherry-Juice' which gives almost miraculous effect in the cases of gout, arthritis and spondilitis. Although less known but wheat-grass juice is held as panacea on the earth. This is supposed to be the best source for obtaining chlorophyll. It also contains other prophylactic and actively nutritious elements in abundance. Let us start with this pancea.

1. THE WHEAT-GRASS JUICE THERAPY

Wheat-Grass Juice Therapy, though coming in global notice not many decades ago, its efficacy was known to mankind millennia ago when man lived like beasts. Whenever hurt, they would apply a sort of grass juice to their wounds. This practice is still prevalent among the aboriginals. What is that especial element in that grass that works wonders. The research pointed it towards chlorophyll for apparent reasons.

In fact wheat-grass like all other type of grasses has abundance of chlorophyll apart from all the minerals essential for body. It also contains Vitamin A 18,000 international units/100g Vitamin C - 100mg/100g,

Vitamin B, E, K and Laetrile-B$_{17}$ etc. Besides these, it also contains carbohydrates, proteins, and fat. Many cancer patients have been cured with Laetrile. But the most vital ingredient of the wheat-grass is chlorophyll. This chlorophyll is contained in a special type of cells called Chloroplasts. chloroplasts produce nutrious elements with the help of sunlight. A famous scientist Dr. Bursher defined it as *"concentrated solar energy."* In fact, chlorophyll is a substance that is present in all green plants. But wheat-grass is perhaps the best source for obtaining plenty of chlorophyll. This chlorophyll has lot of similarity with a substance called hemin which is also found in haemoglobin, an essential constituent of human blood. Haemoglobin contains hemin. From the chemical formation point of view both the substance have many things common. In both of them the arrangement and the number of hydrogen, oxygen and nitrogen molecules are almost similar. There is only one little difference between the constitutions of hemin and chlorophyll. Magnesium is in the centre of chlorophyll molecules while in the centre of the hemin molecules we find iron. Magnesium found in the protons of chlorophyll in essential and beneficial for about 30 enzymes of our body. In the light of this fact, Dr. Wigmore calls wheat-grass a *"green blood."* The following charts represents the chemical composition of the chlorophyll molecules and the hemin molecule.

Chlorophyll molecule
Mg=Magnesium

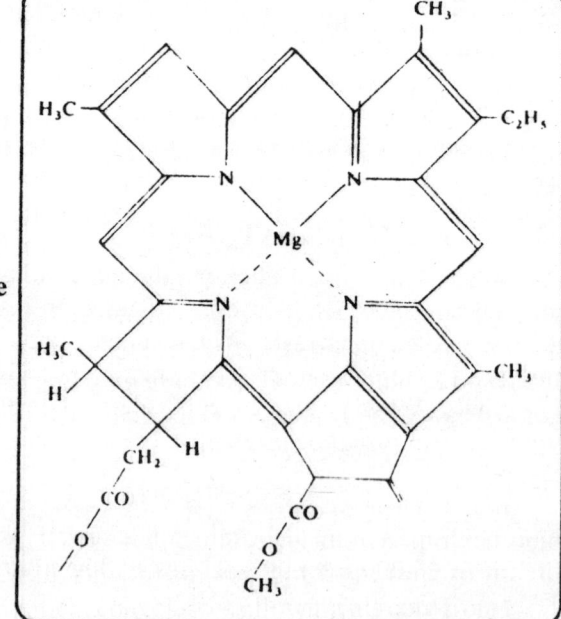

Hemin molecule
Fe=Iron

As we all know the constitution of our blood is a bit alkaline. The proportion of hydrogen molecules (ph) in it is 7.4. Similarly wheat grass is also alkaline and its pH is, too, 7.4. That is the reason why wheat grass is quickly absorbed in the blood and is therefore beneficial to our body. Hence it is perfectly logical to surmise that wheat grass should cure anaemia. We know that anaemia is the state of body in which haemoglobin percentage becomes alarmingly low. It is so because chlorophyll and hemin have similar chemical composition. Moreover chlorophyll is a potent germicidal substance. It destroys certain type of germs that are responsible for spreading certain diseases and paralyses some others which are equally dangerous for us. Taking this quality of the wheat-grass juice in to account many physicians have tried this remedy on a number of ailments such as pyoohea, skin diseases, brain haemorrhage, T.B., heart disease, atherorderosis, tropic ulcer, varicose veins, varicose ulcer, osteomylitis and inflammation of the intestines. Chlorophyll also purifies blood, boosts up the functions of heart and leaves a favourable effect on blood vessels, intestines, lungs and kidneys. It is an excellent tonic as it enhances the basic transformation of nitrogen. The most important aspect to be taken into consideration is the fact that chlorophyll is totally safe and has no side effects. Since wheat grass

contains active chlorophyll in abundance its regimen is capable of curing a host of diseases. The reason why wheat juice is preferred over other herb juices containing chlorophyll are the following :
  (i) Wheat-grass contains a special property that enables to paralyse toxic elements of the body or to eliminate them from the body.
  (ii) Although Alfalfa also contains abundant amount of chlorophyll, it is difficult to grow it in the home as its roots spread deeper in the ground. Besides, after sowing seeds, Alfalfa takes longer time before its grass is ready for consumption. Its taste is also comparatively pungent.
  (iii) The taste of barley grass is bitter. Not only children, but even the elders find it unpalatable to take it for a long time.
  (iv) Paddy grass is generally very dry. Very little juice can be extracted from it.
  (v) Palak leaves juice contains minerals in abundance but very little gastric juice. Some people develop diarrhoea after consuming it and therefore can't take in a larger quantity. Besides that, as it contains oxalates, people suffering from gall-bladder stone trouble should avoid it.
  (vi) Other green-leaf vegetables such as dill leaves and fenugreek leaves also contain medicinal properties, but their taste is generally unpalatable. And secondly they are not easily available round the year.

Taking all these factors into consideration, we can certainly state that wheat-grass juice is safe with no side adverse effects, and is palatable and full of benevolent properties.

TECHNIQUE FOR GROWING WHEAT-GRASS

For growing wheat-grass very big and deep pots are not required. Take seven pots measuring one square feet and having a depth of about three inches. Take only seven pots because after sowing wheat grows to the desired height after 7 days. As a substitute of pots we can also use wooden boxes, lower half of earthen pots, baskets or big tins. If there is a compound or a backyard in the house, wheat can be sowed in small flower-beds or land basins.

Very sticky earth is, however, not desirable for growing wheat grass. Barring that, any other type of earth can be used for growing wheat grass. But do not use the earth in which some chemical fertilisers have been mixed. It is necessary to add some manure to the earth in order to make the wheat grass grow well and acquire some more nutritional elements. In villages, natural manure of cow dung etc. is easily available but in cities where it is not available we can buy packets of readymade compost from the market and use it. But chemical fertiliser should never be used.

For growing wheat grass a better quality of wheat with big grains should be preferred. Wheat grass grown out of big grains is always broad and full of juice. About 100g wheat should be sown at a time. This quantity of wheat gives about 100 gms wheat grass which in turn yields 4 to 6 oz. of wheat-grass. This quanity of juice is sufficient per day for one patient.

Before sowing the wheat, they should be sprouted. For sprouting them, first soak them in water for about twelve hours. Then wrap them in a wet thick cloth and tie them tightly for about another twelve to fourteen hours. As a result of this process, they are sprouted well and shoots appear on them.

Sprouting the wheat grains prior to sowing them is very useful as it is devoid of any germs and you can also anticipate the percentage of the wheat that would grow.

Now spread the sprouted wheat on the soil bed spread them in such a way that the grains remain in touch with one another. Now cover the grains with a thin layer of earth. Then sprinkle some water on it. Remember, water has to be sprinkled only, not to be poured over it. Overdosage of water spoils them altogether. On the wheat grass the water sprinkled should not be ordinary water but the water treated with magnets. This ensures not only the fast growth of the wheat grass but only contains higher amount of nutritious elements. For treating the water with magnet, use the following procedure. Take a glass of water and a pair of powerful magnets (of about 2000 guass each). As we know each magnet has two poles. North pole and South pole. Place the magnet on both the side of the glass in such a way that the north pole remains on one side and on the other remains the south pole. Put a lid on the glass and leave it in that position for about 12 to 15 hours, at the end of which the water is magnetised. When the grass grows a bit high, give water only once during 24 hours. But during summer it might be necessary to sprinkle water 2 or 3 times a day. For giving water to the plant, late afternoon or early evening is generally considered to be the right time. Also ensure that the pots do not remain exposed to the sun light for more than 3 to 4 hours during the day time. When the sun is blazing in the afternoon, keep the pots under a shade. Remember that only one pot per day is to be prepared. Do not prepare all the seven pots at a time. Sow

100 gm. wheat in a pot on the first day. Thereafter, sow 100 gm wheat in a pot everyday for the succeeding six days. On the eighth day you'll find that about 4 to 5 inches high wheat grass is ready in the first pot. So, on the eighth day, from that pot, cut the grass, with a pair of the sharp-edged scissors, as close to the bottom as possible. Extract juice from the grass after washing it properly. Never attempt to pull out the grass from its very roots. Be careful that the wheat grass doesn't grow higher than 4 to 5 inches as the proportion of chlorophyll and other nutritious elements starts reducing from the leaves thereafter. The greater height invariably makes them harder with the juice quantity getting reduced in the process.

After cutting the grass, the earth from the pot should be spread over to allow it to dry in the sunlight. The same earth can be used after about 4 or 5 days. But before reusing it, add some fresh water and manure.

It is necessary to protect the pots and the growing wheat grass from insects, birds and rodents by protecting it with the wooden racks placed in such a way that plants continue to receive adequate air and sunlight. Wrap the legs of the rack with cloth pieces soaked in castor oil or keep them in small vessels filled with water so as to keep ants and other insects of the wooden track. During the summers it is quite likely that wheat grass may not grow well due to heat. So, under such circumstances sow maize seeds instead of wheat and extract the juice of maize grass. This is the best alternative as the maize grass is only slightly inferior to the wheat grass in quality and other medicinal properties.

THE WHEAT GRASS REGIMEN

To derive the maximum advantage of this regimen, first of all the body should be cleared of the existence of the toxic elements. Hence it is essential to start some measures to achieve the best results which include total fasting for a couple of days, taking only water or juices or liquids. Along with these it is also necessary to empty bowls with the help of an enema. During this period only warm water should be taken. Thereafter take only raw food for a couple of days. Raw food may include sweet and sour fruits, sprouted grains, cereals and pulses etc. These measure considerably purgate the body of the toxic elements. Following these measures the wheat grass intake may be launched systematically.

There are two methods of starting this regimen. One is to chew grass and other is to extract its juice by crushing it and taking its juice. Each of these methods has its benefits. These have been briefly discussed below. You may have your choice according to your temperament and liking.

Chewing the wheat grass allows the saliva to mix with it in the mouth itself. Thereby partially starting the digestive process in its very initial stage. After the grass is chewed thoroughly, the residual fibres waste should be spat out. If some of the residual fibres also travel down to the stomach there is no need to get worried, for they, too, are beneficial to the system. Wheat grass fibres prevent and cure constipation. Besides chewing the wheat grass gives the teeth a good exercise and consequently teeth also become strong and clean, as chlorophyll contained in the wheat grass also prevents tooth decay.

Most of the people who launch the wheat grass therapy are generally patient suffering from chronic to serious diseases. They need medicinal substances contained in the wheat grass in abundance. Generally their bodies are a store house of toxic substances due to their faulty eating and living habits. So if those accumulated toxic elements have to be removed quickly it is essential to give them a large dosage of wheat grass. Under such circumstances, it is advisable to prefer administering wheat grass substances to them in the juice form. Compared to solid form, juice can be taken in a larger quantity and that too more easily. It is generally difficult to administer a larger dosage through chewing of the wheat grass. Besides that it is very time consuming too. Very few people have the necessary time and patience to go through this process. Some people even find its taste unpalatable. To chew the grass slowly and allow its juice to go down the throat is often felt to be a boring task by many people. Moreover, the fibrous waste going down along with the juice causes heaviness in the stomach and hempers the digestive process too.

So it is purely the user's choice to adopt to which regimen. There is no harm in shifting mid-way to the other regimen. What is required is a fair and judicious combination of both the ways to get the maximum advantage of this therapy.

THE RIGHT WAY TO CHOOSE THE WHEAT GRASS

Fresh wheat grass, soon after cutting it, should be thoroughly washed first and then eaten. When the fibrous waste turns white in colour, it should be spat out. However, those how are suffering from chronic constipation may also gulp the fibrous waste too. Chewing the grass well is an important factor. In order to masticate out and swallow all the essential substances from the wheat grass it has to be chewed properly and thoroughly.

THE METHOD OF EXTRACTING THE GRASS JUICE

Place the fresh wheat grass, soon after cutting it, on a platform or in a pounding basic and crush it well. Then wrap them in a clean and thin piece of cloth and strain the juice out of it. A plastic strainer could also be used for this purpose. If the magnetically treated water is added to it while crushing it, the extraction of juice will be in a greater quantity with its effectiveness is also strengthened. This wheat grass can be also crushed in the electric juicer or mixer also.

It is necessary to consume the juice of the wheat grass as soon as it is extracted, for if it is left unconsumed for even a few minutes its medicinal properties immediately begin to wane. Some of the volatile substances contained in it turn it into vapour and disappear. Moreover, as the vitamins (particularly vitamin 'C') contained in the juice come into the contact with oxygen in the air and consequently the process of oxidation takes place which makes the chlorophyll also become less effective. So consume the juice as soon as it is extracted.

Remember that this juice shouldn't be gulped down in one go. The juice should be 'eaten' and not drunk. Take a small sip, rotate it in the mouth and gradually swallow the juice. In case you find the juice rather pungent, add a little of grapes or mosambi juice in order to make it soft and more palatable. However, never mix any spice, condiment or salt to make it more tasty as these spices reduce its effectiveness.

DOSAGE

In the beginning restrict the intake of wheat grass or its juice dosage. Gradually it should be increased. In ordinary illness or for a common ailment 100 gm. wheat grass or 100ml juice per day is an adequate dosage. Those who are suffering from some serious or chronic disease should start with 25 to 50 ml per day and gradually increase the intake to 250 to 300 gram or ml. per day.

Even if your disease is fully cured follow the regimen for at least a week. Then you can reduce it to just 50gm. or 50 ml per day for general maintenance. Initially high dosage may cause nausea or diarrhoic conditions. So, keep the dosage or intake low in the beginning and raise it gradually. However you need not be panicky if the above mentioned symptoms appear. Dilute the juice before taking it. In case the complaints persist beyond two to three days, stop the dose for a couple of days and then restart with lesser quantities after the complaints have subsided.

It is advisable to take the juice early in the morning on an empty stomach. After taking the wheat grass or its juice, donot eat or drink anything for about half an hour. The juice gets absorbed in the intestines within half an hour of its taking. Those who find it inconvenient to take it in the early morning can take at any time during the day, when the stomach is empty. But those who wish to obtain the gains of both the methods of wheat grass intake should take juice in the morning only, and should chew the wheat grass at any other convenient hour.

Sometimes in the complicated disease, giving grass juice in very higher dose becomes rather necessary. In that case the juice can also be administered in the body in the form of juice enema also. For doing so, in order to flush the large intestine, take a water enema with some lemon juice added to it. Then after about 10 to 15 minutes, administer about 200 ml wheat juice (about 8 oz) through the enema syringe. Retain this enema in the bowels for about half an hour. In the meantime, most of the juice is absorbed in the bowels and gets mixed with the blood. Thereafter natural call for excretion could be answered, if necessary.

Wheat grass juice has natural anti-septic properties also. Soaked in the wheat grass the gauge can be placed upon the cut or wound, abrasion or a ruptured boil. This juice can also be used in diluted form to wash the germs off the wounds or for the that matter, the body itself. Wheat grass juice gargles yield considerable relief in the throat pain/ inflammation/soreness etc. This juice can also be used to wash eyes. It does help keeping them clean and lustrous.

DISEASES AND THEIR TREATMENT WITH WHEAT GRASS JUICE OR THE GRASS ITSELF.

1. Diseases related to Blood and the Blood Circulation System

Included among this category are anaemia, high blood pressure, atherosclerosis, internal haemorrhage, clotting and the like. Regular intake of the wheat grass juice works wonders especially in the cases of anaemia for which no other therapy has such quick cure. Having 200 ml juice twice a day is recommended.

2. Diseases related to the Respiratory System

Common cold, asthma, bronchitis and all the related disease get cured with the regular regimen of this wheat grass juice therapy. Common cold generally disappears in a couple of days only. Asthma is a dreadfully stubborn disease responding to almost no given therapy. But wheat grass juice taken twice a day creates wonders in this case also.

3. Digestive diseases

Wheat grass therapy is most effective in the case of digestive disorders i.e. it shows its quick effect. Constipation, indigestion, flatulena, nausea, vomiting, acidity, ulcers in the stomach and intestines, smelling on the intestines and worms are some of the prominent diseases and disorders which wheat grass can cure without much ado. However, the patients suffering from constipation are advised to chew wheat grass well at first and then swallow the residual lump also afterwards. If cabbage juice is added to wheat grass juice it yields quicker and better results in the complaint of ulceration in the stomach and intestines.

4. Teeth and Gum related diseases

Wheat grass is an effective remedy for all the complaints of teeth and gums. However, the cure would be butter if wheat grass is chewed and its juice is massaged on the gums.

5. Diseases of Joints

Included in this category are swelling on the joints, pain in the joints, osteorthritis, bone rotting etc. In the treatment of joints the wheat grass therapy has to be employed patiently for long time. However this much is assured that this therapy gives positive results.

6. Skin diseases

As the wheat grass juice is an active blood purifying agent, it is very effective in the treatment of skin diseases. It has been found to be curing eczema, ache (pimples), boils, cuts and wounds, bites and burns. Such patients should take the juice orally and also apply it on the affected parts in the form of a light message Dressing the wounds or boils with a gauge piece soaked in wheat grass juice expedites the healing process.

7. Kidney related ailments

Included in the section are the problem of stone, inflammation of the urinary bladder, and inflammation of the kidneys. Along with the wheat grass juice if water treated with magnets is also taken the results are better and the cure is faster.

8. Disease connected with the reproductive organs

Sexual debility and dismenorhhea are the two disease/disorders which this therapy can cure with comparative ease. Taking the wheat juice orally and applying the parts of the soft portion of the wheat grass on the private parts help greatly cure the disease.

9. Ear diseases

In relieving ear pain and curing the problem of septic discharge from the ear wheat grass juice has shown very good results. In addition to taking the wheat grass orally, some juice should be dropped in the ears to cure ear diseases.

10. **General cure**

Wheat grass juice's administration has been found to o[...] remedy for general weakness, insomnia, headache, fever etc.

Wheat grass juice therapy is an effective remedy even f[...] many other diseases which have not been included in the list given above and therefore it should be given a fair treat in the treatment of all those diseases.

In case you don't find any immediate relief, try this therapy for at least 21 days at a stretch. Only then it can have its full effects. Always remember that such sort of therapy is not like an antibiotic treatment to show its effect immediately. But it does cleans the system better only when you have patience and faith.

2. TULSI THERAPY

Tulsi or Basil is the most hallowed plant specially for the Hindus although Christians also have great sanctity for it. It is a small plant growing to about three to four feet in height. Normally it is grown in pot and kept in every traditional Hindu household for a variety of medicinal and devotional reasons. In fact it is due to its medicinal qualities that have earned for it such a hallowed status. Right from its roots to its branches and inflorescence (Manjari in normal parlance) it is useful in every way. In our rural areas trees and plants are even otherwise an integral part of our everyday life. Among all the trees, shrubs, herbs etc. Tulsi occupies the most respectable and sanctified position. It is worshipped almost as a deity. It is a common sight seeing the Hindu housewife going to light the lamp on the periphery of the pot of Tulsi every evening and watering it religiously every morning. The Hindu scriptures enjoin us to look upon Tulsi not as a mere plant, but as the divine representative of God Vishnu or of Lord Krishna (Lord Vishnu's incarnated form). Tulsi's other name is '*Vrinda*' which go to name the hallowed place near Mathura, called the Vrindavan.

As a matter of fact this reverence for Tulsi is not without some practical reason. Tulsi is the store house of many spiritual, medicinal air-cleaning and even aesthetic virtues. It has variety of uses either for curing a disease or even preventing the onset of ailments and even epidemics. From the point of view of therapeutic effect Tulsi is not merely a healing agent, not merely a medicine but almost a panacea of all physical, mental and even spiritual affections. It is a veritable elixir of life. It has the tremendous power of purifying the atmosphere.

Tulsi has been described as having bitter or pungent taste (its leaves) but this property of it is limited to a peculiar odour and its capacity to kill the germs. A large number of household remedies for day to day afflictions are prepared by mixing Tulsi with dry ginger, pepper, wood apple pulp and the like. Its regular intake has been found to be a sure antidote of malarial affections. It is owing to its these qualities that for a *vaishnav* no *prasadam* is complete unless it has a few leaves of Tulsi spread over the divine eatables. These qualities of Tulsi manifest their effect because of the plant's unusual tenacity to survive in all weathers. It grows in all type of soils. However, the black sticky and moist soil is particularly suitable for it. Its plant doesn't require much care either. Normally its season starts from *Ashadh* (mid-June to mid-July) which peaks on the bright fortnight of *Kartik* (mid-Oct to mid-Nov.) exactly on the eleventh lunar day when its '*marriage*' is celebrated with Lord Krishna in every Hindu household. Following that ritual it is covered with a red cloth (signifying its '*marriedhood*') and remains so during the rigorous winters. It gets dried in summers and regains its verdance again in the rainy season. However, even in its withered state its usefulness remains intact. Even its dry leaves, stems, twigs and roots have their therapeutic usages. In its bloom its inflorescences grows about 2 inch long. Although it is available in many varieties most popular one is the dark-green one, which is called 'Shyam or Krishna Tulsi'. Its other varieties are Drudhriha Tulsi, Ram Tulsi, Babi Tulsi and Tukashmiya. In Sanskrit it is also called Vrinda, Sulabha and Shoolaghni. The botanical name of Tulsi plant is '*Ocimum Sanctum*'. One of the English names for Tulsi is '*the Mosquito Plant*'. Charak, the famous vaidya of the ancient times, describes Tulsi as a cure for coughs, hiccups, poisonous effect and pains in the body. He said that "Tulsi promotes secretion of bile and neutralises phlegm (kapha) and hilious disorders. As it also dispels the unpleasant odours of decaying matter, Charak also claimed it to be '*Pootigandhahaa*' (remover of the smell) due to putnidation. Dhanvantari, the author of '*Nighantu*' has described Tulsi as easily digestible, hot, dry, a destroyer of evil effects of phlegmatic disorders, a killer of worms and stimulant to digestion.

Another property of Tulsi is its 'anti-stress' action. Intake of a few Tulsi leaves or a decoction made of its juice on every day relieves mental stresses generated due to the fast pace of modern life and increases the probability of a long and healthy life.

Tulsi possesses a special kind of vapour which purifies the atmosphere it grows in. Tulsi is particularly effective in combating malaria, and has proved to be the best and easiest means of keeping at bay the insects responsible for the spread of malaria, viz. Mosquitoes. Even snakes can't tolerale the aroma of Tulsi, and keep away from it.

Tulsi plants should be reared in pots and kept in the homes to keep air fresh and pure. Though it is a very common plant, it is an infallible remedy for many major and minor illnesses that are otherwise difficult to cure. It is these qualities of Tulsi that have made it worthy of worship.

Tulsi is being gradually accepted as a valuable therapeutic agent by modern science as well. Western scientists have come to believe owing to a large number of investigations and tests that the Tulsi plant possesses extra electrical energy. This has the effect of keeping the air fresh and pure up to a distance of two hundred meters from a Tulsi plant. This gave rise to a school which claims that the position of a well grown Tulsi plant also ensures that no fall of lightening occurs in the area the plant is placed in.

Since Tulsi has its variety of uses in therapeutic ways and general hygiene, its various medicinal uses have been described below. However it is important that *IN CASE TULSI JUICE IS TO BE WARMED NO HONEY SHOULD BE MIXED WITH IT IN ANY WAY, FOR WARMED HONEY IS POISON, ESPECIALLY IF MIXED WITH THE TULSI JUICE.* As far as possible aged honey should be used in medicinal application and fresh honey for nutritional and in invigorating action.

Another important precaution is for those with hot or hilious temperament. Persons with constitutional 'hot' physiological tendencies or with a tendency to bleed soon should avoid taking Tulsi, its juice or decoction in any form in summers and the initial part of the winters (Oct. Nov.). Also, those suffering from piles should avoid taking Tulsi and black pepper together, as this combination is likely to aggravate the conditions. Also remember that milk taken with all fruits, all sour fruits, meats, garlic, onions, salt, radishes or Tulsi has a deteterious effect in the some special combinations. Whenever it is taken with them, a prior consultation with the vaidya or registered practitioner is necessary.

General Treatment with the help of Tulsi leaves or its Juice

(1) If diluted juice of Tulsi leaves is taken on an empty stomach every morning, it helps in the development of the bodily strength, memory and an impressive personality. Drinking Tulsi decoction with a little sugar (better with sugar candy or '*Misri*') and gives energy and removes fatigue. Daily ingestion of Tulsi juice maintains the digestive efficiency of the stomach and promotes appetite. If Tulsi juice with a little salt in it is dropped into the nostril of an uncon-

scious person, the person quickly regains consciousness.
(i) Tulsi quickly reduces blood cholesterol to normal levels. Daily use of Tulsi removes acidity, cures dysentery colities etc. and is very beneficial in muscular pain, colds, leucoderma, obesity, headaches etc.
(ii) If one takes Tulsi seeds every day with betel leaves, the amount of blood and semen will increase and impotence can be cured.
(iii) As a precaution against malaria, periodic fever and Tulsi leaves with a little of pure ghee and black pepper grains should be taken. The mode of this treatment is very simple. Five to seven leaves are sufficient for children, while adults require 25 to 50 leaves. In case juice of Tulsi leaves are to be taken, grind the leaves on a clean flat stone and squeeze out its juice. Mixer can also be employed for this purpose. Intake of the powder of its '*manjari*' (inflorescences) clears the urine and have an invigorating effect on the body. If fresh leaves cannot be obtained due to their being out of season, the dried and powdered leaves can be substituted instead of the fresh ones.
(iv) It is a good de-addiction dose also. Chewing the leaves with a couple of black-pepper grains whenever the addicted persons (to tea, tobacco or alcohol) feel the urge to have these harmful things is a good course to get rid of the addiction.
(v) Having Tulsi leaves regularly also keeps the body acquire optimum weight, i.e. the thin become sturdy and the fat become lean but powerful.

Tulsi leaves as a remedy to cure snake-bites, stings of insects and the toxic effect of other poisons

(i) Mix Tulsi leaves' juice with hot water and gargle twice every day. It would cure the effect of mercury poisoning.
(ii) In case of snake-bite a paste obtained by grinding together seeds of Aconite, Tulsi, Indrayan, Satodi, 'piludi' and 'black saras' should be applied to the bite with a few drops of it also introduced into the nostrils. The remaining part of the paste should be swallowed by the patient. Alternatively a paste of crushed Tulsi leaves with butter or *ghee* obtained from cow's milk should be applied to the bite of a snake. The paste will darken under the effect of the poison. The darkened paste should be washed off and fresh paste to be applied. Repetition of this procedure will surely draw out the poison. Giving the patient a fistful or two of Tulsi leaves to

chew and swallow will also help. The poison spreading from the bite of a snake can be rendered inactive by administering Tulsi leaf juice to the victim, dropping a little juice into the eyes and ears, and applying a paste obtained by crushing and grinding the roots of the plant at the location of bite. A paste of the crushed inflorescence will also serve the purpose.

(iii) If a person bitten by a snake can quickly (in about 2 hours) drink the juice obtained by crushing and grinding Tulsi, Jatamansi, saffron, turmeric, red sandalwood, *pure manashil, nabhi, tamalpatra,* cinnamon and tagar with sufficient water, he would get cured speedily.

(iv) Applying the paste of Tulsi leaves and roots ground together on the sting of a scorpion with completely eliminate the effects of the poison. Also in such cases, crushing a few leaves of Tulsi with cow's urine and lemon juice, and applying the paste over the region of the sting like an embrocation would cure the problem.

(v) The pain caused by the sting of a wasp can be relieved by drinking Tulsi juice and applying it on the sting.

(vi) The poison of a rat is destroyed by applying a mixture of Tulsi juice and opium.

(vii) To get rid of bugs and mosquitoes, mix Tulsi juice with an insecticide or with kerosene and use the mixture as a spray.

(viii) The poison in a mosquito sting is destroyed by the application of Tulsi juice.

(ix) If by mistake poison of any sort has been imbibed, the victim should go on drinking as much Tulsi juice as possible. This will surely ameliorate the effects of the poison.

TULSI AS A SURE REMEDY TO CURE ALL FEVERS

(i) An incipient attack of malaria can be aborted by taking two or four leaves of the plant crushed with black pepper, or, if suffering from a cold as well, by drinking a decoction of the mixture.

(ii) A malaria patient should be given a decoction of Tulsi roots. This will induce profuse perspiration and bring the temperature down.

(iii) One can be aloof from the malarial attack by taking 10 gms. of Tulsi juice every morning, noon and evening.

(iv) An extract prepared by heating 10 gms. of Tulsi leaves and 10 gms. of '*Amaltas*' pulp in water is an effective cure for all kinds of autumnal or seasonal fevers.

(v) Juice of Tulsi and ginger taken with honey stimulate appetite and help cure colds, fevers, including pneumonia.

(vi) Soak 10 gms of the parts of a Tulsi plant such as leaves, inflorescences and seeds in half a cup of honey or in the '*Mritasanjeevani sura*' (wine) for a week and then strain the liquid. Two spoonfuls of this liquid taken three times a day will cure influenza or all sorts of cold-induced fevers.

(vii) During an epidemic of cholera, burn incense daily in the house and drink only boiled water. Make more liberal use of lemon, onions, garlic, butter milk and Tulsi in your daily diet.

(viii) For fevers due to colds, take the juice of Tulsi leaves with honey.

(ix) Grind 11 leaves of Tulsi, 9 black pepper seeds, 30gms of *ajwain* (Bishop's seeds) and 50 gms of stone ginger in a mortar, and shake well with water. Take a newly prepared dry clay cup or crucible, heat it strongly, and pour the above mixture into it. Then expose your body to the vapours emanating from the hot mixture. When its temperature comes down to a tolerable level, add a little rock salt to the mixture and drink it off. Fever of any type will subside in a very short time.

(x) Taking 10 gms. of the mixed juices of mints and Tulsi leaves sweetened with 5 gms. of crystal sugar is very beneficial in chronic fevers.

(xi) Those who are prone to getting the malarial attacks preceded by cold rigors should drink the decoction prepared by boiling 5 gms. each of Tulsi leaves, mint leaves and ginger.

(xii) Pulverise leaves of Tulsi and those of the dark drumstick tree to a fine powder. This powder taken with lukewarm water cures typhoid fever.

(xiii) Daily ingestion of 10 gms of Tulsi leaf juice is beneficial in typhoid fever and chronic fever.

(xiv) If the fever is accompanied by cough and difficulty in breathing, taking 3 gms. of Tulsi juice and 3 gms. of ginger juice with a teaspoonful of honey. The fever will subside and phlegm will be removed, making breathing easier.

(xv) If there is continuous fever without remission, a paste obtained by grinding two small pepper seeds and mixing Tulsi juice and honey with it, should be taken. This paste is to be licked gradually.

(xvi) A decoction of Tulsi leaves, turmeric and black pepper gives relief in colds and concomitant mild fever.

(xvii) Form a habit of taking 10 gms. of Tulsi juice ground with 1 gm.

of black pepper and 5 gms. of honey.
(xviii) Take 10 gms. of Tulsi seeds, 10 gms. of pepper seeds and 10 gms. of the kernel of '*Karanjalata*' seeds. Grind to a fine paste and prepare pea-sized pills. There pills constitute an effective remedy for fevers associated with abnormalities of semen.
(xix) A suspension obtained by crushing 6 leaves of Tulsi and 7 black pepper seeds with two spoonfuls of water is a cure for typhoid fever accompanied by loose motions.
(xx) In common colds and accompanying fevers, a tea-like decoction of Tulsi leaves is very effective. Take a few leaves of Shyam Tulsi, add some sugar and boil well in a cupful of water. Strain and let the patient drink it with or without cow's milk, as preferred. This treatment continued over a few days will bring the temperature down to normal. The dosage for children would be about one-eighth of that for the adults.
(xxi) Boil five grams of dry Tulsi leaves, 2 gms. of ginger and 2 gms. of black pepper with water. Add milk and sugar. This remedy is ideal for curing fevers and chest pains caused by bound muscles.
(xxii) Chewing 20-25 Tulsi leaves every day during the monsoons and the post rains seasons when respiratory disorders are more prevalent provides protection against these disorders.
(xxiii) Application of the juices of the leaves of Van Tulsi on all nails of the hand and the feet is effective against the lowering of the pulse rate (*Sheetaang*) caused by certain fevers such as typhoid. The treatment should continue a weak more after the cure from the fever.

TULSI AS CURE OF THE COMMON FEMALE DISORDERS

(i) The pregnant women should tie a few leaves of Tulsi round their waist before the delivery in order to lessen the intensity of the labour pains and easing the delivery.
(ii) In case of excessive bleeding two gms of each of the following ingredients should be grind together and its powder should be boiled in 100 gms of water till one-fourth quantity of the water remains. The ingredients are : dry ginger, gum from the bark of a neem tree, *ajwain* seeds, '*tamalpatra*' and equal amounts of the five parts of the Tulsi leaves. The extract should be cooled and then strained. Taking two spoonfuls of it after every four hours would provide relief in the bleeding cases.
(iii) If half a glass of water boiled with Tulsi leaves is taken for each

of the three days starting from the day of menstruation, the probability of conception is greatly reduced. This method of contraception is especially useful as it does not harm the genital organs. On the contrary they become healthier and more potent.

(iv) Itching of the skin over the abdomen and the breasts of a pregnant women is considerably relieved by the application of the paste prepared from the Van Tulsi.

(v) Cumin seeds grind in Tulsi juice and mixed with fresh milk of a cow have beneficial effect in leucorrhoea and they also improve the general health of the women.

(vi) If the menstrual flow is excessive, causing dizziness Tulsi juice mixed with honey will provide quick relief.

(vii) Tulsi seeds soaked overnight for twelve hours in water, crushed well in the morning and administered with sugar relieve the pain following delivery.

(viii) If the women is given a mixture of 20 gms. of Tulsi juice, 20 gms of the juice of maize leaves and 10 gms. of the juice or extract of *Ashvagandha* with 10 gms of honey, her breast milk improves in quality.

(ix) Leucorrhoea can be completely cured by treatment with 20 gms. of Tulsi juice with rice water while sticking to the regimen of the diet of rice and milk and ghee for the duration of the treatment period.

(x) Regular use of powdered roots of Tulsi enfolded in betel leaves stops the bleeding of internal lining of the stomach.

(xi) In the disease connected with the reproductive system of a woman the adhesive property of Tulsi seeds works wonders. The seeds are especially helpful in the cases of amenorrhoea. Treatment with the seeds ground and suspended in water for three days beginning from the first flow of the menstrual flow will help woman to conceive early, since this treatment totally purifies uterus. If an infertile woman continues this treatment for about a year, she will surely conceive. Tulsi leaves specially help make the uterus strong.

(xii) To ensure regularity of the menstrual flow give to the woman the following medicine. Take Tulsi seeds, *naagkesar, ashwagandha, palash* and peepal and ground them to fine powder form, then strain the powder through a fine cloth. Add to this powder 10 gms. of cow's milk and some sugar. Regular intake of this medicine would set right the disturbed menstrual flow.

(xiii) Give the juice of Tulsi leaves (about half a teaspoonful in the evening and morning) to the woman going to deliver soon. This will reduce the intensity of the labour pains.

(xiv) Take 125 gms. each of the following ingredients : Tulsi seeds, black seasame seeds, tender shoots of the cotton plant and tender shoots of bamboo plants, and add a bit of aged jaggery to make the whole lot converted into small balls or pea-sized pills. If these pills are taken one at a time with water every morning and evening, they will surely restore the regularity of the menstrual flow.

TULSI AS CURE OF THE COMMON MALE DISORDERS

(i) Application of the following paste in a thick layer on the scrotum is beneficial in the treatment of hydrocele. Take leaves of Tulsi, '*hadiakarshan herb*' and '*amarbel*' and add them with the droppings of camels. Grind all the ingredients to a paste form and apply as indicated above.

(ii) In case of difficulty in or stoppage of urination, drinking Tulsi juice with double its quantity of grape juice, sugarcane juice or coconut milk will induce profuse urination.

(iii) A drink prepared by soaking 10 gms of Tulsi seeds overnight in one cup of water, mashing them well in the liquid and adding sugar will relieve dysuria.

(vi) The following treatments have been found especially efficacious in curing dysuria: Take 10 gms. of Tulsi leaves add 5 gms of water and cow's milk and take the potion twice daily. Alternatively dysuria can also be relieved by drinking a mixture of 10 gms. of Tulsi juice and 10 gms. of Lemon juice. Chewing a few leaves of Tulsi daily for a few days in also beneficial in curing dysuria.

(v) For nocturnal emissions the following treatments have been found especially effective.

   (a) Soak 10 grams. of Tulsi leaves overnight in water in an earthen pot. Grind them well in the morning with 15 almond kernels and 16 small cardamoms. Add sugar (preferably sugar candy) to taste and drink the mixture in the morning and evening.

   (b) Chew a few pieces of the Tulsi leaves folded in a betel leaf after meals to prevent nocturnal emissions.

   (c) Take 10 gms of '*Sudhamooli*' 10 gms. of Tulsi leaves and four bits of cardamoms. Boil them together after grinding them to a paste form. Strain and cool and have two spoonfuls of it every morning and evening.

(vi) **The problem of adequate sperm-count** : This problem in colloquial parlance is also known as thinness of the seminal fluid. Powder 50 gms. of Tulsi seeds and 60 gms. of sugar together. Take 5 gms. of this powder with cow's milk every day. Alternatively, take 50 gms. of Tulsi leaves, 40 gms. of 'musali', 40 gms. of the pods of '*poshi*', 30 gms. of '*kavach*' seeds, 50 gms. of gokharn (small caltrops) and 60 gms. of sugar. Grind all these together to a powder and strain it through a fine cloth. Take 10 gms. of this powder with cow's milk every day.

(vii) **The problem of premature ejaculation**
  (a) Cut Tulsi roots into thin slices. These slices taken with betel leaves increase the power of retention.
  (b) 5 gms. of powdered Tulsi leaves taken with betel leaves are also beneficial.
  (c) Two gms. of a mixture obtained by crushing Tulsi roots and Jimikand (elephant yam) together, taken with betel leaves will also help control the trouble.
  (d) Take 50 gms. of Tulsi seeds, 40 gms. of 'musali' and 60 gms. of crystal sugar, and powder them together. 10 gms. of this mixture taken with cow's milkk everyday will improve the quality of the seminal fluid and prevent premature ejaculation.

(viii) **The problem of Gonorrhoea** : Also called '*Sujak*' (in hindi) it is urinary disease related to chancroid. This disease is treated in the following manner: Take 5 gms. each of Tulsi seeds, seeds of small cardamoms and nitre and powder them together. Have 5 gms. of this powder and wash it down by diluted milk. (1:2 milk, water ratio). Drink this potion as many times at possible. Make sure that no sugar or any other substance is added to it.
Alternatively, prepare a smooth paste by grinding Tulsi seeds with a little water. Boil the paste with twice its amount of neem oil. Allow the mixture to be boiled till the paste is blackened by the heat. Now cool the oil, separate from it the charred particles and apply the oil on the sores. This oil is very efficacious to cure all sorts of sores and wounds.

(ix) If there is pain and a burning sensation in the urinary passage while passing urine, prepare a mixture of 125 gms. of milk, 125 gms. of water and 20 to 30 gms. of Tulsi leaf juice, and drink it up.

(x) Soak 5 gms. of Tulsi seeds overnight in 125 gms. of water. In the morning, mash them thoroughly and drink the suspension. Regular and continuous use of this preparation will prove beneficial in gonorrhoea, thinness of the seminal fluid, dysuria and allied diseases.

(xi) Mix Tulsi seeds and jaggery. Roll into pea-sized pills. If one of these pills is taken every morning and evening with cow's milk for four months, there will be a definite enhancement in the production rate of semen and the blood vessels shall also be strengthened. This treatment also improves digestion and restores potency of even a totally imbecile man.

(xii) Ground with cumin seeds and sugar and taken with milk, Tulsi seeds becomes very efficacious in the treatment of pains caused by stones in the bladder, burning sensation while passing urine and inflammation in the perineal region.

(xiii) Taken with honey, crushed Tulsi seeds cures all the abnormalities in the genital system including nocturnal emissions and help greatly in checking gonorrhoea.

(xiv) Tulsi seeds' regular consumption eliminates pain accompanying urination.

(xv) Take powdered Shyam Tulsi mixed with lemon juice regularly to cure all uro-genital defects.

(xvi) Soak 10 gms. of Tulsi root powder overnight in a cupful of water. Grind it well in the morning, mix will and strain the suspension. This dose taken daily can cure even gonorrhoea.

(xvii) Take with milk collected straight from the teats of a cow (*Dharoshna*) Tulsi seeds' powdered form and add a little old jaggery with it. This will also improve the quality of the seminal fluid. However, it is essential that the treatment should continue for 40 days.

(xviii) Take a few Tulsi leaves dried in shade and crush them to a fine powdered form. Add to it powdered *methi* (fenugreek) seeds and powdered *Ashwagandha herb*. Take the whole mixture with cow's milk to check gonorrhoea. It also adds to the thickness of the seminal fluid.

(xix) An effective dose to cure nocturnal emission is taking equal amounts of powdered. Tulsi leaves. '*Sheetal Chini*' (cubebs) powder and camphor with cold water at the time of going to bed.

(xx) Mix with 100 gms. of Tulsi leaves 20 gms. each of '*chopchini*', taseemphana, peeparimool, nagkesar and akkalgaro (palatory root). Grind each of these separately to a fine powder, and soak each one in old honey, using in all 200 gms. of honey. Keep it acide for 24 hours. Now prepare a thick syrup of 500 gms. of white (refined) sugar. Allow it to cool. Then stir the soaked ingredient along with the honey into the syrup. Now grind 100 gms. each of saffron, seeds of small cardamoms and 'Javitri' (mace) to a fine powdered form. Add these powder also to the syrup, stir well and store in a glass jar. If 10 to 20 gms. of this preparation are taken regularly with cow's milk sweetened with sugar, adjusting the amount according to the state of your health, this dose would greatly help in improving the quality of your seminal fluid and other allied genito-urinary problems. While undertaking this course observe strict celibacy.

(xxi) Taking five parts of Tulsi plant with crystal sugar would go a long way is restoring your sexual debilities curing a variety of the allied genito-urinary problems.

TULSI : AS A CURE FOR DISEASES OF CHILDREN

As Tulsi is a very mild and harmless substance it is ideal for treating the diseases of children. Many of the children disease's and disorders such as fevers, coughs, regurgitation of milk, difficulty in breathing etc. get cured quickly by this Tulsi based treatment.

Normally Tulsi juice should be warmed before it is given to children. Just 2 to 5 gms. of Tulsi seeds will suffice in most of the juvenile disorders. As a tonic administration of Tulsi juice is recommended to the children which keep them healthy and the threatened disorders at bay.

(i) In fever and common cold cases Tulsi juice should be smeared on the chest and forehead. The child should be made to inhale the varpours emanating from the juice. Along with it, half teaspoonful Tulsi juice with equal amount of honey (old) should be given to the sick child.

(ii) If there be worms in the child's system, occasionally visible through vomit and faeces, give him 10 gms. of Tulsi juice with a little of *vayuviding, kakcha or himej* for two to three days to make him get rid of the trouble.

(iii) In case of dry cough, the child should be given tender shoots of Tulsi and ginger crushed together and mixed with honey. Ask the child to lick the paste and not swallow it with water.

(iv) Rubbing a bit of Tulsi juice on the child's gums before teething would help the teeth appear without much difficulty.

(v) If Tulsi juice is administered in the initial stages of colds, fevers, accumulation of phlegm, vomiting or diahorrhoea, these problems would be cured easily.

(vi) In the cases of dry cough, prepare the following extract. Take 5 gms. of Tulsi inflorescences, 5 gms. of *vaj peepar* (sweet flag) and 20 gms. of crystal sugar and boil them in 500 gms. of water until half of the water remains. Now strain and cool the extract. Give, one teaspoonful extract four to five times to cure the trouble.

(vii) In case of normal cough administer a mixture of five gms. of Tulsi leaves, five gms. of *Kakdashingi* and five gms. of *'ativish'* buds crushed together, made into a paste with honey and mother's milk.

(viii) *Kasondara* leaf-juice given with Tulsi leaves' juice is a tried and tested remedy for coughs.

(ix) Boil 10 gms. of Tulsi leaves, 10 gms. of methi seeds and 5 gms. of *'Kadu'* twigs in 50 gms. of water till only one-fourth of the water remains cool and strain. Administration of this extract is very beneficial in fevers preceded by cold rigors such as malaria.

(x) A child would instantly get relief from abdominal pains, a slightly warmed of Tulsi and ginger juices will provide relief.

(xi) Thirty to sixty drops of the following mixture administered two to three times a day to a child suffering a cold or cough will prove greatly beneficial to the child in cases of cold or cough. Take 5 gms. each of Tulsi leaf juice, *ajwain* seeds and turmeric and ground to a very fine paste in mortar. Add to it 25 gms. of honey, mix well and store the mixture in a glass container. Give 30 to 60 drops of this mixture to child twice or thrice in a day.

(xii) If a baby's abdomen is distended due to the accumulation of gas, the condition can be relieved by giving to it 5 to 10 gms. of Tulsi juice, adjusting the amount in accordance with the age and constitutional build of the child.

(xiii) In the case of the diarrhoic conditions accompanying the teething trouble of a child, give a little of the Tulsi leaves with half the quantity of the juice of a pomegranate.

(xiv) To a child troubled persistently by cold and cough give him a little of Tulsi juice with honey twice or thrice a day to bring instant relief.

(xv) In case you baby is suffering from colic pain, give him a little powered stone (dry) ginger (sauntla) with Tulsi leaf for quick relief.

(xvi) An infant, being fed on breast milk, should be given three drops

(xvii)   of Tulsi juice mixed with honey to lick if he or she get bouts of vomitting and retching.

(xvii)   If an infant, being fed on breast, suffers from cold or cough, brew tea for him with four to five leaves of Tulsi and give this tea twice or thrice to him/her for quick relief.

(xviii)   Massaging the gums with Tulsi leaf juice mixed with honey will help the baby cut its teeth easily without the usual troubles associated with teething.

(xix)   Five to ten drops of Tulsi leaf juice given with water every day will strengthen the muscles and bones of the infants.

(xx)   Take equal amounts of Tulsi seeds, nagar moth, 'atees', Kakadashingi, stamens of flowers of the smaller variety of kateri (chitraphala), vayviding, roasted cumin seeds, the smaller variety of peeper bamboo manna (vansa lochan) and saffron. Grind them together to a paste and form into small pills of the size of green grams. If these pills are given to a child every night for four or five days, most of the diseases including diarrhoea, difficulty in breathing, dyspnea, cough, vomitting, dacryocystitis, excessive movement of the ribs due to strain in breathing etc.

(xxi)   In order to get relief the child cases of influenza and coughs administer 30 to 60 drops of a mixture of 15 gms. of Tulsi leaf juice, 15 gms. of honey, 5 gms. of ginger and 5 gms. of powdered *Ajwain seeds*

(xxii)   Fevers and coughs can also be cured by giving the child 10 to 30 drops (according to its age) of a suspension of 2 gms. of black pepper powder in 15 gms. of Tulsi juice in which 5 gms. of crystal sugar has been dissolved.

(xxiii)   If there is a wheezing sound heard from the breathing of a child, apparently caused by the accumulation of phlegm due to exposure to cold winds, the child should be given milk in which Tulsi leaves have been boiled. Then cover the child with a blanket to keep the body warm. Soon the condition of the child will improve.

(xxiv)   Relieving the diarrhoea of the child during the teething period add two gms. of powdered Tulsi seeds in breast milk or in cow milk and administer the dose through the child's mouth.

(xxv)   Warmed Tulsi juice would get the child relief from the worms.

(xxvi)   The extract of Tulsi roots sweetened with sugar will relieve constipation and distension of the stomach, also ensuring a satisfactory bowel movement.

(xxvii) Take equal parts of Tulsi and betel juice, heat the combination a bit and give it to the child to provide it relief from flatulence caused by indigestion.
(xxviii) Grind 10 gms. of Tulsi leaves and 10 gms. of 'peeper' together to a paste form. Then form small sized pills. Three or four of these pills given to a child everyday will cure coughs including whooping cough.
(xxix) An extract of Tulsi leaves and inflorescences given with jaggery to a child will provide relief to children having difficulty in breathing. Also giving 3 to 5 gms. of Tulsi juice to the child according to its age.
(xxx) If your child is prone to vomitting, powdered Tulsi seeds given to him will cure the trouble.
(xxxi) Powdered bark of Tulsi roots given with honey helps an obese child to shed some of the fat.
(xxxii) Extract of Tulsi is an effective remedy for liver disorders of children.
(xxxiii) A few drops of warmed Tulsi juice in the ear will relieve earache of children.

SOME SPECIAL TREATMENTS WITH TULSI AS THE BASE

In order to cure *'Vata'* disorders (caused by the disturbance in the 'humour-wind' of the three basic humours according to Ayurvedic school) Tulsi has been found to be very effective. If there are neuralgic pains due to excessive formation of *'Vata'*, Tulsi decoction has been found to be very efficacious. Specially the *'PANCHANG'* of Tulsi is very useful. It is the five parts of Tulsi, the roots, leaves, inflorescences, twigs and seeds of the plant. Take equal amounts of these parts, grind them together, and pass through a fine mesh. Ten gms of this mixture mixed with an equal amount of old jaggery and taken with goat's milk every morning and evening will quickly relieve pain in the joints. Also, Tulsi juice mixed with powdered black pepper and pure ghee is an effective remedy for the inflammation caused by the wind-trapped in the body. Repeated administration of 5 gms. of a mixture of the juices of Shyama tulsi, garlic and onions, and smearing the mixed juices all over the body is beneficial in tetanus as well as spasms due to other causes.

An ideal cure for all conditions due to excessive vata such as pains, inflammation etc. is the following. Take 5 gms. of Shyama Tulsi, 3 gms. of mendi *(sindhur)* leaves, 5 gms. of bhangra and 3 gms. of the bark of *'Varuna'* and convert all the ingredients in to powdered form. Take this powder with 5 gms. of honey.

Normally Tulsi juice and ginger juice's combination come in as a handy treatment for curing the disorders related to *'Vata'* problems. Another effective treatment for this kind of disorders is an extract prepared by boiling Tulsi leaves and the roots of the castor plant. The extract is to be allowed to cool and should be taken with honey.

For pains in the flanks and other pains caused by vata a good remedy is applying the warmed paste prepared by grinding Tulsi juice, ginger juice and the powdered roots of *Pushkar* together.

The use of decoction of Tulsi leaves for bathing and fomentation of the joints is effective in the treatment of rheumatism. Tulsi seed powder is even alone a good remedy for curing muscular pains.

Another treatment to cure vata related disorders is exposure to the smoke generated by DrudribTulsi leaves dropped on glowing charcoal which proves beneficial in all cases of abnormalities of blood due to Vata, including oedema of the hands and feet.

Rheumatoid arthritis can be cured by fomentation with steam from water boiled with Drudib Tulsi leaves and drinking the decoction when it cools to bearable temperatures.

Also take *Panchang* of Tulsi (five parts of the Tulsi plant), *panchang* of neem, *panchang* of *kateli* (a variety of the cotton plant), leaves of white sindhur, leaves of the 'Amar bel' and black makay (maize) and cook 125 gms. of the paste in seasame oil over a low flame. When all the moisture is expelled, cool and strain the oil. Use this oil, to massage the joints and other parts getting troubled by rheumatism.

Try the following tried and tested remedy for the treatment of hemiflegia (having half the body inactive). First of all wash the affected parts with and extract of the panchang of the Tulsi plant. Prepare an extract of the leaves, roots and flowers of the following five plants. Tulsi, neem, bilwa (wood-apple), Inderjau and 'ganiari'. Massage the affected parts with the extracts while it is still fairly hot. Also drink suitable quantities of the extract at given intervals.

TULSI : FOR IMPROVING MEMORY

(i) Swallow five leaves of the Tulsi plant with water every morning.
(ii) Crush together 8 to 10 Tulsi leaves, 4 to 5 black pepper seeds, 2 to 4 almonds and little of honey. Regular ingestion of this preparation greatly improves the powers of the brain.

TULSI : AS PURIFICATION AGENT

Just drop a few leaves of green Tulsi and wait for some time. Then strain the water and drink it—It is now totally safe.

TULSI : RECOVERY FROM AN ELECTRIC SHOCK

If a person has received an electric shock either by touching a wire carrying an electric current or by lightning, massage the face and the head of the victim with Tulsi juice. This would soon revive the person's consciousness.

TULSI : AS A SOOTHING BALM ON THE BURNS

Smear the affected part with coconut oil that has previously been boiled with Tulsi juice. This will reduce the pain and will hasten the subsidence of the blisters and the healing of the wounds.

TULSI : A DE-ADDICTION AGENT FOR THOSE ADDICTED WITH CHEWING PAN (BETEL LEAVES)

We must have come across many persons addicted to this dirty habit. The habit of constantly chewing betel leaves results in weakening of the gums and deterioration of the teeth. Tulsi leaves can be used to free oneself from the habit. If you are addicted to the habit of taking betel leaves after meals or even inbetween, you may take the betel leaves but follow it up by chewing a few Tulsi leaves. This will not only clean your mouth but shall also kill the urge to have more betels. In fact in Sri Lanka there is a tradition of using Tulsi leaves instead of the betel leaves and eating them after applying a bit of *catechu and lime*. This would not only be helpful in de-addicting your dirty habit but also improve your digestive system.

TULSI : AS A CURE FOR EVEN CERTAIN HEREDITARY DISEASES

There have been certain bodily disorders that are called hereditary disorders which are generally held to be incurable. Prominent among these is asthma and diabetes. Most of the schools of medical treatment claim that one has to live with it as there is no treatment. However, Tulsi raises a ray of hope for such patients. It is clearly stated in *'Padmapurana'* that if the woody trunk of Tulsi or clay in which a Tulsi plant is growing is rubbed like sandalwood on a flat stone and the resulting paste smeared regularly on the forehead, the process of arresting the hereditary ailments begins which does cure those ailments to a very great extent.

TULSI : THE BEAUTIFYING AGENT

Tulsi has inherent beautifying qualities besides being an anti-septic substance which make it especially useful for this purpose. Start your beauty-treatment with Tulsi in the following manner: Early in the morning, after your bath, spread a mat in the proximity of a Tulsi plant and sit in such a position as to allow the fragrance emanating from its leaves, inflorescences and stem to mix with the air you inhale. Inhale deeply and hold your breath. Let the maximum amount of the fragrance enter your lungs with the air inhaled through the nostrils. Let this fragrant air laden with salubrious chemicals penetrate your body as deeply as possible. Let it permeate in every part of your body. This divine aroma will purify your blood. The purified blood will impart a glow to your body and give it a new lease on life. It is said that its fragrance alone is very effective in increasing the beauty, health and radiance of the body. No wonder the Gopis of Vrindavan were peerless 'beauties' since they lived in the cluster of the Tulsi leaves.

Even otherwise Tulsi is considered to be an efficacious remedy to cure leucoderma and other skin disorders. Rubbing finely powdered dry Tulsi leaves on the face like talcum powder makes it glow with beauty. This powder will also remove light and dark spots on the face.

Tulsi leaves purify blood. Chewing a few leaves of the plant will purify your blood and turn it bright red. This in itself will improve your looks. Again applying a thick paste formed by crushing and grinding dry Tulsi with a little pure water to the face opens up the pores of the skin. The dirt in them is easily flushed out of the pores through perspiration, leaving the skin glowing, soft, clear and free from odoriferous substances, thus imparting radiance to the face.

For retaining the natural freshness of the skin of the face, try this formula : Take some water in a vessel. Squeeze half a lemon into it. Now add a fistful of Tulsi leaves, a handful of mint leaves and boil it. Now cover your hair and expose only your face to the steam emanating from this water. Apply some of the water to your face when it has cooled down to a bearable temperature. If there are dark spots on your face, add some lemon to the juice of Tulsi leaves and apply this mixture on the spots. Let it dry and then wash it off with clear water. If this is done regularly every morning and evening, the spots will disappear in a few days and the face will become clean, fresh and glowing. An equal amount of ginger juice can be substituted for the lemon juice.

Prepare a face-pack with Tulsi as the base in the following way : Keep lemon juice for twenty four hours in a copper vessel. Add the same amount of Tulsi juice and *kansandi* juice (This fruit is easily obtainable from any perfumery. It is also called *Kasaunji or harfa revdi*,.

Thicken the mixture by evaporating it in sunlight. Apply this paste to the face. Leave it for about 10 mts. and then wash it off with lukewarm water. Apply it for a couple of days and see how your face acquires a new, glowing look. This paste is also effective in the cases of black heads.

TULSI AS SKIN CURE AGENT

(i) Boil Tulsi leaves in oil of *sarson* (mustard). When the leaves turn black and charred, take the oil off the fire and strain it. This oil is beneficial in all skin diseases.

(ii) In the cases of scabies, ringworm, eczema or pruritis, drink Tulsi juice and apply it on the affected parts. Use a decoction of Tulsi leaves for bathing.

(iii) Dry Tulsi leaves in the shade, add some alum, grind well and sieve through fine cloth. Store the powder in a clean dry glass bottle. This powder can be applied on any fresh cuts or wounds, and will promote quick healing. Since Tulsi is itself anti-septic, don't worry for any untoward aggravations.

(iv) Application of Tulsi juice on boils is quite beneficial and gives relief.

(v) In eruptions or areas of locally swelling tissues caused by *'Sheeta Pitta'* (urticaria) apply Tulsi juice over the affected areas. This should be followed by daily application of crushed Tulsi leaves mixed with black clay. Also, application of Tulsi leaves ground in water from the river Ganga makes skin eruptions subside in a very short time.

(vi) Boils in the armpits come to a head, burst and heal, on application of a warm poultice of Tulsi leaves, mustard seeds, jaggery and googal (Mukul) ground together.

(vii) Pain due to burns is alleviated by applying equal quantities of Tulsi juice and coconut oil mixed well. Blisters and wounds caused by the burn will also heal quickly.

(viii) Tulsi leaves and roots prove beneficial in the treatment of almost all skin diseases because of their powerful anti-septic properties. Grind 200 to 250 gms. of Tulsi leaves with water, and squeeze out the juice by pressing them. Boil 250 gms of this liquid with 250 gms. of seasame seed oil. When all water has been boiled off, strain the oil and store it in a glass bottle. Massage with this oil cures a large variety of skin diseases including itching.

(ix) As Tulsi has a purifying action on the blood, it can be used to cure all diseases caused by abnormalities of the blood, such a blisters, boils, furuncles, eruption etc. Take 50 gms. of lemon juice in a copper vessel. Add 50 gms. of Tulsi juice and the same quantity of juice of black 'Kasondra'. Keep the vessel in sunlight. The Juices will begin to lose water by evaporation. Expose the vessel to sunlight daily till all the water is lost and a dry residue is left. The residue will be almost black in colour. Application of this residue all over the face not only cures acne, black spots and other similar disorders, but also improves the appearance and beautifies the face. Treatment with this powder also cures white spots on the skin due to leucoderma.

(x) Ringworm can be cured by applying a paste formed by grinding Tulsi leaves and leaves of the lemon tree with curds.

(xi) White spots on the face or any other areas of the skin are commonly called 'spiders'. Apply the clay adhering to the roots of a Tulsi plant on the affected parts immediately on rising in the morning, even before cleaning your mouth. The improvement will be evident in a few days.

(xii) In cases of quick hair loss and baldness, rubbing the skin of the head with Tulsi leaves and powdered *Anwala (emblic mynobalan* fruit) would provide very quick and beneficial results. Even the hair would also turn black and the hair-loss will be stopped.

(xiii) Application of Tulsi leaves grind with red clay is an effective remedy for ringworm.

(xiv) A festering wound exuding puss and blood will stop oozing and begin to heal if a paste of ground Tulsi leaves is applied. Also treatment of a wound with a powder consisting of equal parts of Tulsi and camphor destroys the microorganism infesting it.

(xv) Drinking the juice of Tulsi leaves to which white (refined) sugar has been added is greatly beneficial to the patients of leprosy. The kind of leprosy spreading downwards *(Adhogami)* gets great relief if finely powdered Tulsi roots enfolded in betel leaves are regularly taken.

(xvi) The *'gajakarna'* leprosy can be successfully treated by applying a will-stirred homogenised mixture of ghee, lime, Tulsi juice and betel leaf juice.

(xvii) Twenty gms. of Tulsi leaves ground with one clove of garlic yield a paste application of which quickly cures ringworm.

(xviii) Drinking the juice of the leaves of Ram Tulsi regularly proves beneficial in serious diseases like leprosy, if the treatment is con-

tinued for the period about a year.
(xix) Drinking van Tulsi juice is effective in removing or fading the marks left on the face by small pox infection.
(xx) In cases of dracontiasis, apply the paste obtained by rubbing Tulsi roots on a flat stone on the spots on the skin that are itching. This will have the effect of causing the worm-like organism to come out to the extent of two to three inches. Wind this portion of the worm on a suitable piece of twing like a thread in the usual way, and apply the paste again the next day. Repetition of this treatment for two or three days will cause the whole organism to emerge. The resulting wound would heal completely if the same treatment is continued.
(xxi) Itching and eczema can be cured by applying a paste obtained by prinding the leaves of a Tulsi plant in lemon juice.
(xxii) An easy cure for prickly heat eruption is eating Tulsi seeds crushed with Anwala fruit jam.
(xxiii) In the case of tetanus drinking the juice (five gms.) of garlic, ginger, onions mixed with the leaves of Shyama Tulsi gives quick relief. The juice of the mixture may also be applied all over the body for better results.

TULSI : AS TEETH-CARE AGENT

(i) Chewing Tulsi leaves two to four times a day after meals will clean the mouth, remove bad odours emanating from the mouth and clear the bad taste in the mouth due to fermentation of the residual food particles. This will also prevent the urge to have paan-masala, betel leaves etc.
(ii) Take decoction of the *panchang* (five parts) of the Tulsi plant, add a little of warm water to it and gargle twice a day to prevent the disorders of the teeth like decay and crevices etc.
(iii) In case of toothache rubbing the teeth with the juice of Tulsi mixed with black pepper provides immediate relief.
(iv) Placing a pill made from the paste of Tulsi leaves under an aching tooth will also alleviate the pain. Pills rolled from a paste prepared by grinding black pepper with the juice of Tulsi leaves are also effective.
(v) To prevent the teeth decay with the help of Tulsi prepare the tooth powder in the following manner. Take the Panchang of the Tulsi plant, betel nuts (supari) and almond shells and roast them in a pan till they are charred black. Then powder the whole lot. Fifty

gms. of this powder, then, should be mixed with a finely powdered mixture of 10 gms. of black pepper, 10 gms of camphor, 10 gms. of alum, 10 gms. of *mulethi (yasteti madhu)* and 10 gms. of peepal catechu. Brushing the teeth with this powder every morning will reset loose teeth firmly in the gums. This powder is very effective to check pyorrhoeas and other ailments of the teeth.

(vi) Chewing Tulsi and chameli leaves helps in the cases of mouth ulcer. Brushing the teeth with the Tulsi juice also helps.

TULSI : AS EYE-CARE AGENT

(i) Prepare a decoction of the leaves of Shyama Tulsi and dissolve a little of alum *(fitkari)* into it. Then strain the liquid. If wads of cotton are wetted with this decoction and placed on the eyelids, eye strain is relieved together with swelling of the eyelids also subsided and vision improved.

(ii) Night blindness can be cured by instilling two drops of the juice of Shyama Tulsi leaves into the eyes every day for fourteen days.

(iii) Dropping Tulsi leaves juice into the eyes relieves soreness of the eyes and is also beneficial in other eye disorders. Tulsi leaves, juice mixed with honey, strained and stored in a glass bottle constitutes excellent eye-drops medicine.

(iv) Prepare a decoction of Tulsi leaves and dissolve some powdered alum in the decoction. If there is inflammation or itching of the eye-lids, warm this decoction and use cotton dipped into it to format the eye-lids. During the fomentation change the cotton wads twice in every five minutes.

(v) Prepare a decoction of Tulsi leaves and dissolve some powdered alum in the decoction. If there is inflammation or itching of the eye lids, warm this decoction and use cotton dipped into it to foment the eye-lids. During the fomentation change the cotton wads twice in every five minutes.

TULSI : AS THE EAR-CARE AGENT

(i) Take enough of Tulsi leaves and cook them in mustard oil. When the leaves have blackened due to charring, take the oil off the fire and strain it. Put a few drops of this liquid into the ears if there be any earache due to cold weather/infection etc.

(ii) Boil Tulsi leaves and whole (unbroken) seeds of black pepper in til (seasame) oil, and strain the oil. Instilling this oil into the ears cures deafness, and suppuration of the ears.

(iii) Mix Tulsi juice with seasame oil and boil the mixture. A few

drops of this oil instilled into the ears while bearably hot will cure all disorders of the ears.
(iv) Instillation of a mixture of equal amounts of the juices of Shyama Tulsi leaves and *Bhringraj* is an effective treatment for infection of the internal ear and consequent suppuration.
(v) Earache, inflammation of the inner ear and deafness are cured by regularly instilling drops of the mixed juice of Green Tulsi inflorescences and Tulsi leaves.
(vi) Instilling van Tulsi Juice is also an effective cure for deafness.
(vii) Instilling Tulsi leaf juice into the ears will cure earache including sharp, shooting pains in the ears. If there is pus formation the ears should be first cleaned with two drops of Tulsi juice put into each ear. This should be repeated every morning and evening. If the need be, the juice may be warmed a little before putting it into the ear.
(viii) Maize (*Makka*) leaves and Tulsi leaves combination is also good to relieve the earache.

TULSI : AS A NOSE-CARE AGENT
(i) If a boil or a furuncle has formed in the nose, inhalation of a pinch of dry powdered Tulsi leaves like the snuffing powder will cure it.
(ii) If the nasal passage is infested with micro-organism due to decryo cystitis with consequent emanation of bad odour, the vapours from a mixture of Tulsi leaves juice and camphor should be applied.
(iii) To get rid of the pain or furuncle in the nasal passage, a mixture of powdered Tulsi leaves and powdered kernels of the stones of the '*Jujube*' (ber) fruit should be inhaled, and the mixed powder should also be applied on the affected area.
(iv) In case of nosebleed swelling the fresh Tulsi inflorescences brings immediate relief.
(v) If the nasal infection has made the throat also sore, lick the Juice of Tulsi leaves mixed with honey for quick relief.

TULSI : A PANACEA FOR HEAD AND HEART PROBLEMS
(i) Take 5 gms. of Brahmi herb leaves and 5 gms. of Tulsi leaves. Crush them and strain their juice. Have it twice a day for keeping hysteria neurosis etc. at bay and also improving your memory.
(ii) Applying the paste of sandalwood mixed with a few drops of Tulsi is a sure remedy for relieving mental tension. (Tulsi is also called 'shoolagni' for its inherent anodyne qualities).
(iii) Inhaling smoke formed by putting the Van Tulsi inflorescence on

       live charcoal cures headache speedily.
- (iv) Dropping a few drops of any Tulsi into the nostril of an unconscious person would quickly revive his consciousness.
- (v) Taking Tulsi leaves crushed with a few seeds of black pepper is a very good brain tonic. Add a bottle of honey and a couple of Almond kernels to make the tonic much more efficacious.
- (vi) Take 4 gms. of the bark of 'Arjun' tree with 2 gms. of powdered Tulsi to strengthen your heart nerves.
- (vii) Honey mixed with Tulsi leaves is a good decongestant agent to dilute the deposits of the cholesterol on the walls of arteries.
- (viii) Taking 6 leaves of Tulsi with six grains of black pepper on empty stomach for 21 days helps check the epileptic fits. (The same combination, if taken before retiring for the day is an ideal dose to combat consinophelia and bronchial disorders. This treatment, however should be continued for three days. Moreover, Tulsi leaves, shouldn't be consumed as it is during the period body is hot with high temperature).
- (ix) Sandhav salt, Tulsi juice should be taken together to cure the brain weakness manifest in fainting.

TULSI : AS A REMEDY FOR BLOOD DISEASES

- (i) Tulsi is highly effciacious remedy for anaemia. Regular use of Tulsi effects a very rapid increase in the number of the red blood corpuscles.
- (ii) Those who have white corpuscles in the blood suddenly rising, as is manifest in the cases of eosinophelia or other chronic disorders of the brochial chord, taking 6 leaves of Tulsi with 6 grains of black-pepper is very effective. But these shouldn't be swallowed but chewed without taking water no matter how uncomfortable one feels due to the pungency of the black-pepper. Then the person should sleep fully covering himself (or herself) in a blanket or some other sheet. The whole idea is that the body heat shouldn't be allowed to escape. Continue the treatment at least for three days. It is a tried and tested remedy. But it shouldn't be resorted to when one is down with high fever or the body fever would be enhanced.

TULSI : AS AN EFFICACIOUS REMEDY FOR TB

      In ancient times, '*Yakshma*' (as TB was known in olden times) was not only cured with Tulsi treatment but there used to be Tulsi sanatoria to make the patient convelesce following his cure from the TB affliction. These sanatoria had Tulsi Vans (small forests of Tulsi) around them. There were sanitary huts, the walls and floors of which were plastered with clay which had the Tulsi plants growing in them. The sole aim of this plaster was to ensure that the TB germs shouldn't get a foothold in the vicinity of the patient. It is believed that the volatile oil present in Tulsi leaves destroy these germs. For it is a fact that things exposed to the aroma of Tulsi or placed near a Tulsi plant will not deteriorate or get spoiled quickly. Perhaps the religious ritual of putting Tulsi leaves in the mouth of a dead person had this thought in its origin.

TULSI : AN ANTI-DOTE OF CHOLERA AND OTHER EPIDEMICS

(i) Van Tulsi is a wonderful anti-dote for cholera. Take 20-30 gms. each of the following ingredients. Tulsi leaves, kernels of the seeds of '*Konaji*', the bark of the neem tree, '*adheji*' seeds, *guruchi* (oozing fluid) from the neem tree, and Indrajan. Boil them in half a litre of water till half the water has been boiled away. Give the cholera patient 20-30 gms. of this extract at short intervals.

(ii) During an epidemic, arrange to administer one spoonful of a mixture of juices of Tulsi leaves and neem leaves to every member of your family twice every day—once in morning and once in the evening. This would keep your family under a protective cover from that epidemic's ouslaughts.

(iii) Swallowing five leaves of Tulsi every morning also protects one from infectious diseases. (Care should be taken to ensure that they donot come in contact with the teeth, as such contact will harm the enamel of the teeth).

(iv) Tulsi leaf's juice sweetened with sugar is a good preventive for sunstroke, and if one is already afflicted with the sunstroke, the drink will assist recovery.

(v) Breathing in the vicinity of a Tulsi plant cures diseases of the lungs and strengthens the lungs.

(vi) Drinking an extract of Ram Tulsi leaves with cow's milk and sugar removes fatigue instantly, and almost reinvigorates the body.

TULSI IN PREPARATION OF SOME SPECIALLY POTENT POTIONS

Tulsi Tea : It is a very efficacious potion and quite popular with various institutions having even western genesis. It is prepared the following way : Wash 20 to 30 leaves of Tulsi, and pound them to a pulp form. Mix this pulp with a cupful of water. Spice the mixture with proper amounts of powered dry ginger, cardamom seeds and roots of peeper (piper longum). Add a spoonful of sugar and boil. Drink this decoction while still hot. Never strain the decoction. Chew and swallow the cooked pulp of Tulsi leaves after drinking the decoction. Take it daily instead of tea. This is believed to be capable of curing various diseases, and stimulating the appetite. In winter it is a sure anti-dote against all cold disorders. If an extract of Tulsi leaves is prepared as described above, an equal amount of milk is mixed with is, and 10 to 20 gms. of powdered '*Sudhamoli*', a few powdered seeds of cardamom are also added to it, you get a highly nutritious drink is obtained.

Alternatively, take 1500 gms. of Tulsi leaves dried in shade. Add 500 gms. of *brahmi roots*, 1 kg of *tamalpatra*, 1 of powdered sandalwood, 1500 gms. of aagia grass, 250 gms. of cinnamon, 1 kg. of saunf (aniseeds), 125 of 'banafshah' and 500 gms. of cardamom seeds pulverise all these to a fine powder, and store in a glass jar. When you want a hot-drink from above mentioned powder, boil 500 gms. of water, add 10 to 15 gms. of this powder and continue to boil till a homogeneous fluid is obtained. Strain the liquid and add sugar and milk according to your taste. This tea is highly beneficial in fevers, coughs, colds, excessive secretion of phlegm and disorders of the vocal or bronchal chord.

Tulsi Sat : Grind six to eight leaves of Tulsi with three four black pepper seeds in a mixer with a littler water till a homogeneous thick liquid is obtained. Drinking a glass of such a cold extract of Tulsi every morning on an empty stomach soothes the brain and provides it strength. This drink also has very good effect upon heart. In case you want you can add peeled and pulverised almonds also with it to not only improve its taste but render it more potent. However such addition are desirable only during the winters.

Tulsi Pak : Tulsi leaves and its inflorescences are very good for making tasty and salubrious sweet-cake. For this use Shyama Tulsi leaves which are abundantly available in the month of Sept-Oct.

Pound or grind Tulsi seeds to a fine powder like flour. Before beginning the preparation, keep the following ingredients ready. Tulsi seeds, flour, 125 gms. black pepper seeds, 10 gms. bhang (canabis), 5 gms., saffron 2 gms. almond seeds, 125 gms.; khoya 125 gms. bengal gram flour 125 gms. crystal sugar, 250 gms. ghee (clarified butter) 250 gms.

Mix about three-fourth of the ghee with the gram flour. Sprinkle a little milk over the flour. Take the remaining portion of ghee in an iron or brass pan and put it on the stove. When the ghee is fairly hot, add the gram flour and let it cook in ghee over a low flame. When the flour is nearly half cooked break up the khoya into small lumps, mix it with the gram flour, and continue heating till both the khoya and flour have been fully cooked, and start turning brown. Now add the almond seeds, cut into small pieces, and let them cook for some more time. Now add the Tulsi seeds-flour. Immediately after that add the bhang powder, Cardamom and pepper powder according to your taste, mix well, and take the pan off the fire.

In the meantime prepare a thick syrup and add saffron to it. The thickness of the syrup should be adjusted to suit weather conditions. It should be a bit thicker in the monsoon otherwise the sweet is liable to be spoilt early and become soft due to moisture in the air.

In the winter, on the contrary, the syrup shouldn't be made so thick and viscous, thicker syrup results in greater hardness of the sweet. If it is desired to increase the proportion of ghee in the sweet so as to increase its nutritive valve, somewhat thinner syrup will do. Once syrup of proper consistency had been prepared, add the saffron and mix the roasted flours in the syrup with constant stirring. Now the delicacy is ready. Spread it in a flat plate white it is still hot and allow it to set in. When it is comparatively hard, cut it in to the pieces of desired size and shape. This sweet is an ideal tonic for the persons of weaker constitution. Two pieces (nearly 50 to 100 gms.) would be an enough diet which should be washed down with 250 gms. of hot milk. This not only enhances your physical, sensual, sexual powers but also strengthens your nerves.

Tulsi Ghrita : This is a medicated ghee prepared with the Tulsi base which is very effective in curing most dreadful skin diseases like leprosy and leucoderma. For this first grind 125 gms. of Tulsi leaves and 125 gms. of serpent stone (*guruch*) with about 750 gms. water. Add 500 gms. of cow's ghee and boil the mixture till it becomes fully homogeneous. Strain and cool and preserve in a glass jar for application on the body every morning and evening.

CHPATER VI

FRUIT AND VEGETABLE THERAPIES

THE DIFFERENCE BETWEEN FRUIT AND VEGETABLE

The basic difference, for a layman, between fruit and vegetable is that which could be consumed raw is fruit while that could be consumed raw as well as cooked is vegetable. Botanically speaking fruit is the ripened ovary of a flower, either by itself or in combination with other structures that have matured with it as a single organic unit. Although this definition again refers to both fruit and vegetables, the term 'vegetable' in its broadest sense refers to any kind of plant life or plant product. It usually refers to the fresh edible portion of a herbaceous plant consumed either raw or cooked. The edible portion may be a root like beet, carrot, a tuber or storage stem like potato or calacosia; the bulbs such as onion and garlic, a leaf such as cabbage, lettuce, spinach or an immature flower like cauliflower, a seed like pea or green grams or an immature fruit like brinjal, cucumber or mature fruit such as tomato or chilly. There is also a difference. Those plants or parts thereof that are usually consumed with main course of a meal are popularly regarded as vegetables while those mainly used as desserts are considered fruits.

These form an essential item of our diet. Vegetables supply some elements in which other food material are deficient and they neutralise acid substances produced in the course of digestion of meats, cheese and foods prepared with rich animal fats like ghee. The dark green leafy vegetables are rich source of carotene which is converted by the body into vitamin A. Vitamin C is also richly provided by leafy and green vegetables.

There are also some vegetables which are valuable sources of proteins or carbohydrates. Beans and peas are also rich in iron and protein, while potatoes are important sources of carbohydrates. It is an established fact that cooking and heat destroys nutritive value of the vegetables. Hence it is advisable to consume vegetables in as much raw state as possible. There are some vegetables like carrots, beans, spinach, turnip, cucumber, tomato, garlic, onion etc. which are mostly consumed raw although they are cooked also. This school believes that most of the diseases are caused by our having vegetables etc. not in the form they are produced. Over 2,400 years ago, Hippocrates, the father of medicine, said : "*Let living (natural) food be thy medicine.*" It is now being increasingly felt that we can get all the necessary nutrition for our body through our consuming only uncooked food. It has enough of vitality to ensure our healthy survival. Cooked food is considered as dead and actually unsuitable and unsage for the human body.

Drugs and operative methods on the body come and go. But fruit juice therapy has survived and flourished through the ages because of its unique benefits. Fruit juice therapy is very strong and effective as it removes the defect from the root. It has got no side-effects after-effects. It does not damage any part of the body as drugs do. Since they have no narcotic effect they don't addict you. Nature has provided us with some life-saving fruits like *mausambi*, orange, garlic, onion, payaya, cucumber, bittergourd etc. As we know that toxins are the main cause of diseases we can't get get rid of them unless we start taking raw fruits and vegetable juice. It is for this purpose we have selected a few chosen vegetable and fruit therapies for the benefit of our discerning and enlightened readership.

1. GARLIC THERAPY

Also called *Lehsun* or *Rashun* in colloquial parlance, botanically it is called *Allium sativum*. It is a bulbous perennial plant of the lily family which is generally used for flavouring foods. Its aroma is powerful and taste is pungent. Its bulb contains antibiotic allium and it has antiseptic properties. It is also an expectorant and intestinal antispasmodic. Garlic has been in use since hoary past and the oriental Haqueems called it *Lehsun Badshah* (the emperor). It is believed that there are only six possible 'Rasas' and it alone contains five of them. It is probably one of the most powerful antiseptic known to man. Catarrh simply can't persist against garlic. All kinds of worms get destroyed by garlic. Garlic contains Vitamin A, B, C and D in plenty. Chemically it contains calcium, iron, phosphorus, iodinc acrolein (which kills germs) crotonic aldehyde, allyl sulphide and volatile terpenes.

According to pauranic legends, Lahsun originated from drop of nectar dropped from sky in a scuffle between Indra and Garuda and so it is also called Amritodbhava. It is called Rasas because it contains all Rasas except the Amla-rasa (bitter sour flavour). Lahsun plant is a delicate plant 1 to 2 ft. in height, with long, cylindrical leaves which surround the stem bearing white flowers (inflorescences). It has:

Carbohydrate	29.00%	Protein	6.3 %
Fat	0.1%	Mineral Salts	1.0 %
Volatile Oil	0.06 %	Phosphorus	0.31 %
Lime	0.03 %		

In the following way it is used to cure the diseases:

(i) **Asthma**
   (a) Lahsun juice taken with hot water twice a day.
   (b) One fried shellot (*Kali of Lahsun*) with little salt twice a day
   (c) 10 drops of *Lahsun* juice with 2 teaspoon of honey is reputed to be curing asthma. It can be attacked at the time of attack also.

(ii) **TB (Tuberculosis) of Lung**

Lehsun or Garlic should form the staple diet of such patients because garlic is rich in sulphuric acid which has the capacity to destroy the TB germs chewing 10 shellots of garlic boiled in 250 gms of milk and then having that milk immensely helps in curing TB. Also swelling cotton wool soaked in Garlic juice would take the aroma to the lungs to help them get rid of TB.

(iii) **Heart Problem.**

Garlic is especially helpful in dissolving the cholestrol. Having milk with a few garlic shellots (*kali*) boiled in it plus having garlic in your food is especially helpful. In case your system is not very hot, you can have two shellots of garlic on an empty stomach. This can be easily done in winters and rainy seasons. Avoid it in case of hot temperament during the summers.

(iv) **Paralysis**

Having garlic kheer (shellots of Lehsun boiled in milk till it grows thick. Then add sugar, cool it and have it) regularly brings quick relief. Also apply garlic juice on the affected part/parts. The oil for this massage is prepared the following way. Boil 250 gms. ground garlic shellots with 500 gms mustard oil in an iron Karhahes (pan) till it is burnt. Put some camphor in it. Cool it, and keep it for massaging the body every morning and evening.

(v) **High Blood Pressure**

Hypertension gets reduced if 6 drops of garlic juice is mixed with fresh water and the potion is drunk every morning.

(vi) **Bronchitis**
Paste of garlic with onion applied on the chest as pontice roots out all the infection of the bronchal chord.

(vii) **To quell the tridosh disturbance**
Tridosh means all the three basic humours of the body (bile, phlegm and wind) getting disturbed. For bile—use ground garlic paste with sugar added as chutney with your food for quick relief.

For phlegm—add garlic juice with honey and lick the mixture twice or thrice a day.

For windy problem—Have garlic juice mixed with ghee (especially during rainy season).

(viii) **For any kind of cough and cold problem, including the whooping cough**
Regular intake of 3 to 5 shellots of garlic cures common cold and cough troubles.

To get rid of whooping cough mix 6 to 7 drops of garlic juice with a cupful of pomegranate juice and have the mixture for a few days. This treatment will automatically cure all kinds of cough and cold troubles.

Whooping cough is also cured by having one shellot of garlic with soaked, peeled and ground almonds (2 pieces) and *Misri* (sugar candy) in the morning.

All kinds of coughs get cured by having 8 to 10 drops of Lehsun juice with half spoonful of honey at least three to four times a week.

Five drops of garlic juice mixed with a cupful of hot water quells even the most violent cough bouts.

(ix) **Sore Throat**
Gargles with hot water with few drops of Lehsun mixed in it would cure this problem quickly.

(x) **Sneezing**
5 to 7 shellots of Lahsun with hot water taken once stops frequent sneezing.

(xi) **Malaria**
Application of garlic juice on nails of hands and feet before fever and taking 1 tsp garlic juice with 1 tsp fresh water thrice a day cures malaria.

(xii) **Jaundice**
4 ground shellots of garlic mixed with half cup hot milk for 4 to 5 days helps curing jaundice.

(xiii) **Impotence**
Keep 200 gms. ground garlic mixed with 600 gms. pure honey in

a bottle which should be kept in a wheat of sack for about a month time. Then have regularly chapatis made of this flour. Alternately take 10 gms. of garlic paste and wash it down with lukewarm milk. Continue that treatment for about a month to get back your manliness. Also, chewing 4 shellots of garlic slowly early in the morning followed by drinking luke-warm milk or taking ghee-regularly in winters give extraordinary strength to men and it also removes fertility in women.

For men having problem of involuntarily or uncontrollable discharge, chewing 1-2 shellots of Lehsun with one cup hot milk before bed-time thickness their semen and cures the trouble.

(xiv) **Migraine**

Paste of garlic applied on forehead or near the ears for 3 to 4 minutes and putting a couple of drops of garlic juice in the nostril (of the affected side) considerably relieves the pain of migraine.

(xv) **Earache**

Boil garlic juice (a few drops) with half teaspoonful of mustard juice instantly relieves earache if it is caused by cold winds or even some infection.

(xvi) **Gastric ulcer and acidity**

Taking a tiny ball (about ½ cm. in diameter) of the ground garlic paste after you have taken a few sips of plain water following your meals would remove acidity and heal up ulcer. But remember to drink more water after taking the garlic paste.

(xvii) **Diarrhoea**

If the diarrhoea conditions have set in due to any infection taking 2 to 3 shellots of garlic with water has a soothing effect on the various types of diarrhoea.

(xviii) **Flatulence, Sciatica**

Small dose of decoction of garlic, given three or four times a day cures both the problems. The decoction is made by straining and boiling together 6 ounces of garlic with 2 pints of water and 4 pints of milk till the liquid remains half of its quantity. Once its water has evaporated and can be strained and cool. Have a spoonful of its at six hourly interval.

(xix) **Worms**

Taking a garlic shellot with water following your food relieves this trouble speedily.

(xx) **Urinary Problems**

Paste of garlic applied below the navel relieves strangery and induces profuse urination.

(xxi) **Pynorrhoea**

Boil garlic shellots (4 to 5) in a cupful of mustard oil. When garlic gets fried-strain the oil, cool it and mix it with fried and ground 30 gms. of *ajwain* seed and *sendha* salt. Use this liquid to brush your teeth with.

(xxii) **Baldness**

Apply a little of garlic juice on the bald head. Then have it to get dry. Do so at least thrice a week. This would not only stop the falling of hair but shall revitalise the hair growth on the bold patch.

(xxiii) **Dog-bite and similar problems**

Paste of garlic applied on the better part quickly counteracts the poison. Also grind 5 to 7 shellots of garlic and mix with ½ pint of milk. Make the victim drink it as soon as venomous bite takes place.

General precaution about using all the decoction pastes etc. made with garlic is the quantity of garlic in it. Use only the recommended quantity. In case it becomes more it may produce flatulence headache, nausea, vomitting etc. As a local stimulant and irritant, it reddens the skin and may cause vesication. So don't leave it applied on the skin for more than a couple of minutes.

Garlic might cause some problems to a pregnant woman as it has a tendency to charge the body. Hence garlic or its preparation should be administered to or applied on a pregnant woman under medical supervision of a competent practitioner.

2. AMLA (EMBLIC MYROBALANS) THERAPY

Botanically called *Emblica officinalis*, it is a rich source of vitamin C, amino acid, tannin, polyphenolic compounds, fixed oil, lipids and other essential oils. It may be compared with *'Amrita'* (nectar) of the heavens owing to the medicinal qualities of this divine fruit. Its regular consumption is an anti-dote for many ailments/disorders like acidity, septic fever, biliary colic, vomitting, insomnia, defective vision etc.

Amla tree is found in all parts of India. It is generally 20-30 ft. high. Its bark is rough and brownish in colour. It has regular branches, bluish yellow flowers, small leaves like that of the *Imli* (tamarind) tree. Its fruit is round and greenish yellow in colour with six segments and a hard seed inside. Among all the varieties that are available, the best is Kalami for its fruit has lot of pulp, very small seed and is comparatively less sour and bitter in taste than others. It is especially good for making jams, pickles, chutneys etc. Chyavanprash is also made from Amla only.

Perhaps owing to its medicinal qualities the Hindus treat it is a very sacred tree and worship on '*Akshaya Navami*'. In the Kartik month (mid Oct. to mid Nov.) if one takes its dose regularly it provides complete protection against all the disorders due to cold. Amla is unique as it doesn't leave its chemical ingredient even if it is heated. It is a tree whose no part is useless. It also has the atmosphere purifying qualities.

Chemically, besides being the best source to get Vitamin C from, it also has gallic acid, tannic acid, sugar, albumen, calcium, protein, phosphorus, carbohydrates, irons etc.

AMLA AS GENERAL TONIC

Taking Amla and Black Til in equal quantity with honey or ghee cures mental and physical weaknesses.

To revitalise brain take a cupful of sugarless milk with the murabba of Amla.

Taking even one raw Amla every morning even with water makes one's body enough resistance to fight with various ailments.

Taking milk in the morning after licking one teaspoon of ground Amla powder mixed with honey imparts freshness and strength to the body. Intellect get sharpened if one takes the pulp of fresh Amla or Amla juice with honey or ghee every morning and evening.

AS AN EYE TONIC AND CURE OF EYE AILMENTS

Washing eyes with cool water having Amla powder soaked and strained is good for the eyes and it also improves eye-sight.

Washing the eyes with ground Amla and til powder water (soak Amla and Til powder in water overnight and strain it) in the morning cures burning sensation in the eyes.

Applying pulp of Amla on the head and washing the hair after massage helps in curing burning sensation in the eyes and heaviness of the head.

Have Amla powder washed down with milk to improve your eye-sight.

Eating 10 gms. of *Triphala* (the powder made by mixing even quantity of Harar, Bahera, Amla powders) with 1 tsp of honey keeps eyes very healthy strong and sparkling.

Having Triphala powder with honey not only keeps eyes bright and shining but it is also very good for the digestive system.

FOR CURING HEAD AND HEART AILMENTS

Taking Amla Murabba every day in the morning cures physical and mental debility. Taking Amla juice is ideal for keeping your head and eyes strong.

Massaging the scalp with Amla oil before going to bed removes mental weakness.

Taking Amla powder with cow's milk or *Misri* (even amount) with water gives relief in heart ailments.

Applying paste made up of dried Amla powder with Kumkum, Neelkamal and rose-water cures headache. Applying paste of Juice of 2 to 3 Amla or its pulp mixed with little rose water and 3 to 4 pieces of kesar (saffron) in it—on the affected part for 15 mts. relieves the pain of migraine.

CURING INVOLUNTARY NOCTURNAL EMISSION

Taking 10 gms of fresh Amla juice with 1 gm. of powdered *haldi* (turmeric) and honey every morning and evening cuers this problem.

Taking Amla water (soak dried Amla powder in 1:3 proportion in water for 12 hours, strain the water and mix 1 gm. haldi powder) regularly helps in curing night discharge problem.

PROBLEMS CONNECTED WITH URO GENERATIVE SYSTEM

Taking 1 gm Amla powder, kala jeera and 2 gms. ground misri with cold water cures the problem of bed wetting.

Taking milk after eating fresh Amla juice or dried Amla powder with *gur* (jaggery) cures stranguary.

Applying paste of Amla near the naval portion helps in curing urinary problem. Boil 20 gm. pulp of dried Amla in 160 gms. water till 40 gms. is left. Then mix 20 gms. of Gur (Jaggary) in it. Drinking this potion helps in urinary problem.

Taking crushed Amla pulp (after straining it) mixed with *misri* cures blood in urine.

Taking 20 gms fresh Amla Juice with 10 gms. of honey and water twice a day cures problem connected with urination.

ACIDITY AND DIGESTIVE PROBLEM

Licking one tea spoon of dried Amla powder with honey or ghee after dinner checks acidity.

FEMALE AILMENTS

Taking 3 gms. powdered Amla with 6 gms. honey every day for one mouth cures the problem of leucorrhoea.

Leucorrhoea is also cured by taking powder of Amla seed with honey or misri regularly. Taking 20 gms. fresh Amla juice mixed with honey regularly for a month cures weakness of the generative system.

BLOOD IMPURITIES

Taking Amla juice or powder with honey purifies blood.

Taking 5 gms. of powder (made from 20 gms triphala, 20 gms. black pepper, 10 gms. pure sulphur, 5 gms. of neem leaves and mehandi leaves—ground in fine powder form) with a glass of water twice a day cures all impurities of blood.

DIABETES

Taking fresh Amla juice with honey checks diabetes.

PILES

Soak 15 gms. Amla and 15 gms. of *mehandi* (myrtle) leaves overnight in 400 gms. water strain the liquid in the morning. Drinking this water checks piles. Taking 5 gms. of triphala churna with a glass of whey helps in curing piles. Also, taking fresh Amla juice with half tsp of ghee and 1 tsp. of honey and 100 gms. of milk—after lunch—cures even chronic piles problem.

STONE-PROBLEM

Taking Amla powder with radish helps in checking stone in bladder by breaking the stones and throwing it out with urine. The best time to have them is morning or evening.

CONSTIPATION

Have 1 tsp dried Amla powder with milk or water before retiring for the day. It helps in imparting movements to the bowels and keeping the system clean. Also taking strained water of mashed fresh Amlas soaked overnight in lukewarm water helps in evacuating the bowels. Taking 4 tsp fresh Amla juice and 3 tsp honey mixed in a glass of water relieves constipation. If constipation is caused by worms, take about 20 gms. fresh juice of Amla every day to kill the worms.

COLD AND COUGH

Taking two tsp of fresh Amla Juice with honey twice a day helps in taking out the phlegm and controls cold. Also, taking milk in which a little Amla powder and ghee boiled in the evening helps in dry cough. Licking Amla powder with honey regularly twice or thrice a day also cures chronic dry cough.

SKIN TROUBLES

If there is the problem of extreme dryness of the skin, taking tea boiled with pieces of Amla in it mixed with sugar and milk helps greatly. Itching problem is cured by applying Amla churna in chameli oil (dry Amlas in shade, powder them and mix them in chameli—Jasmine oil. The bottle should be kept in shade) on the part of the body where itching is gives reting.

BALDNESS AND OTHER ALLIED PROBLEMS

Washing the head with Amla-juice mixed with water after rubbing the scalp for 10-15 mts. with fresh Amla juice helps in restoring the vitality of hair. Soak dried Amla, Harar, Bahera and Shikakai in an iron utensil overnight and mesh them nicely, washing your hair regularly with this strengthens the hair and checks hair loss.

Applying the paste of Amla powder mixed in lemon juice on the hair 10 to 15 mts. before washing them with Amla water keeps the hair strong and shining.

Dying the hair with the following herbal paste makes them turn automatically black and strong. Make the paste of Amla and Mehandi leaves and apply it on the hair. Keep it applied for about 15 to 20 mts. Then wash it off with lukewarm water. This will make your hair black and shining.

Washing the hair with dicoction of Amla removes dryness of the scalp, checks dandruff and stops excessive fall and the greying of hair.

Massaging the head with Amla oil imparts natural glow to hair, relieves mental tension and induces sleep.

JAUNDICE

Soak 4 *Munnakkas* (big raisins) in juice of 4 fresh Amla. After one hour grind the soaked munakkas and mix it with Amla juice. Taking this potion twice a day gives relief in Jaundice.

Mix a churna in the following way. Grind each of Amla, dry ginger, black pepper, 3 gms. of iron bhasm and little turmeric. Lick this churna mixed with a teaspoonful honey helps cure Jaundice.

GOUT

Taking fresh Amla juice with old ghee—heated a little—regularly for a few says relieves stiffness of joints and helps in curing gout.

REMOVING THE SPOTS LEFT BY MEASELS, CHICKEN POX, SMALL-POX ETC.

Take bath with the water having Amla juice mixed in it. Also, apply the paste made of Amla and til in equal quantity ground in cold milk added with 3 or 4 drops of rose water on spots and let it stay for sometime and then wash it off with Amla soaked water.

BOILS IN MOUTH

Doing gargles with water having fresh Amla juice twice or thrice a day gives great relief and helps curing the boils. After gargles apply fresh Amla juice on the boils and let saliva ooze out.

LICES IN HAIR

Applying the paste of ground seeds of Amla mixed with lemon—especially on the roots of the hair and washing after half an hour will clear the lices from the hair. Even when washing it off use the water having little of Amla juice.

AMLA AS THE BEAUTIFYING AGENT

Application of the Amla paste mixed with turmeric and—oil on—body makes the skin clear, soft and improves the complexion.

Drinking Amla juice mixed with honey in the morning makes the compelxion glowing and blemishless.

Application of the Amla paste on the face and washing it off after 10 to 15 mts class pimples and heals up the spots so created.

CHECKING MENSTRUAL DISORDER

Take boiled pulp of Amla with honey two times a day relieves the pain in the bleeding.

Taking Amla juice mixed with ripe banana 3 to 4 times a day during periods—checks profuse bleeding.

INSECT-BITE

Applying the paste made of *Triphala* powder mixed with cow's urine—on the affected part—relieves the poisonous effects of insects.

Drinking Amla juice will also help in such cases.

GENERAL MAINTENANCE OF HEALTH

Munching raw Amla or one piece of Amla Murabba washed down with milk is an ideal breakfast for staying healthy and living till ripe old age.

Also, taking Chyavanprash (heaving enough of Amla) in the morning is also very good tonic for maintaining good health.

Taking *sharbat* of Amla in summers keeps the body cool even in the height of summers.

3. LEMON THERAPY

Botanically called '*Citrus Medica*', it is a small tree or spreading bush of the rue family (Rutaceae). The lemon forms a spreading bush or a small tree 10 to 20 feet high if not trained or pruned. Its young leaves have a decidedly reddish tint, later they trun green. In some varieties, the young leaves of the lemon are angular, some have sharp thorns at the axilae of the leaves. The flowers having a sweet odour, are rather large, solitary or in small clusters in the axilae of the leaves. Reddish tinted in the bud, the petals are white above and reddish purple below.

The humble lemon contains most of the vitamins and minerals. It has magical and wonderful healing powers. It is the chief source of a citrus acid. All citrus fruits are very rich source of vitamins A, B, and C. They also contain appreciable amounts of iron and calcium. It is chiefly the vitamin C which makes lemon such a wonderful fruit capable of scoring scores of the physical and medical troubles singlehandedly. Vitamin C in the diet helps the body to grow and maintain collagen. The researches reveal that collagen is a gelatin like gristle that holds billions of cells together in the body. It is found in ligaments, joints, bones, gum tissues and in the walls of all the blood vessels. It also gives elasticity and strength to the connective tissue. Again vitamin C is necessary to the normal healing rate of wounds to prevent bruises from discolouring the skin for too long time. Its function is also to strengthen the body's resistance to infectious and maintain tissue integrity of teeth, bones and gums. Since vitamin C is the most vital requirement for all the person, given below is the chart giving its optimum requirement of all age of people every day.

Men 75 mg, women 70 mg, lactating women 150 mg, pregnant women 100 mg, infants 30 mg, children (1 to 3 yrs.) 35 mg, (4 to 6 yrs.) 50mg, and 7 to 9 yrs 60 mg, boys 75 mg, (10 to 12 yrs.) 80 mg, (13 to 15 yrs.) 100 mg, (16 to 20 yrs.), girls (10 to 12 yrs.) 75 mg, (13 to 15 yrs.) 80 mg, (16 to 20 yrs.) 80 mg.

Amount of vitamin C in the following fruits :

Whole orange	75 mg
4 oz. orange juice	50 mg
Large grape fruit	150 mg
Lemon Juice (1tbl.)	7 mg
Lime (*Mausambi*)	75 mg

Vitamin 'C' is needed by the body for the following reasons :

(i) As an antidote to the damages caused by smoking and alcoholic beverages.

(ii) To counteract the stress and strain and fatigue caused by busy life.
(iii) To do quick repair to the wear and tear caused by injury and diseases.
(iv) To counteract the process of aging.

Lemon juice cures menorrhagia, nose-bleeding, hepatitis, gastric ulcer if taken several times daily. Of all foods which have also been used as medicines, lemon is the most commonly known. The custom of using a slice of lemon when eating a fish dinner was originally intended for remedial purpose rather than for flavouring. It was believed that if a fish bone were to be accidently swallowed during the meal, the juice of lemon could dissolve it. Lemons have been used as a household remedy for colds, rheumatism, sore throat, gastric and liver troubles, headache, heart burn, biliousness etc. Lemon juice mixed with glycerine is used for chapped lips or chilbrains. For constipation, the juice of a lemon is taken in a glass of hot water one-half hour before breakfast. Local application of lemon juice is also used for various types of skin cares.

USE OF LEMON JUICE IN VARIOUS DISEASES

(i) **Rheumatic and Bone-Related Diseases** : A few drinks of lemon juice is the surest remedy for rheumatic fever, painful joints, lumbago and sciatica. This would involve no cardiac complication. Those with incipient arthrties were given ascorbic acid therapy (lemon juice therapy essentially) and positive results were achieved.

(ii) **Cough and Cold** : Roasted lemon when properly prepared is one of the most effective remedies for cough and cold.

(iii) **Corns** : Apply lemon juice few times a day and see the miraculous results. Bind the corn and leave it overnight and get rid of the trouble soon.

(iv) **Common cold** : Lemon juice taken three or four times a day along with garlic or ginger juice cures such troubles speedily.

(v) **Oedema** : Oedema of the muscular region produced by vascular demcompensation often responds more rapidly when 10 to 33 ounces of orange or grape-fruit juice is given in addition to 500 mg. of vitamin C for three to four days.

(vi) **Prickly heat** : An age old remedy, taking lime juice diluted with water a few times in a day, ensures relief from it.

(vii) **Cardiovascular diseases and hypertension** : Person suffering from these problems must have lemon juice at least a couple of times in a day. In case they can, they should also have a few drops of garlic and honey added to this potion. Taking a glassful of luke-warm water with a few lemon juice drops squeezed in it ensures quicker relief from such disorders.

(viii) **Menorrhagia And Haemorrhage** : Have a few drinks of lemon juice or *narangi* (orange) juice will surely give some relief in acute menorrhagia.

(ix) **Asthma** : Having half-teaspoonful of lemon juice, washing it down with luke-warm water before each meal provides quick relief to Asthma. Repeating it as the last dose of the day and starting the day with it also gives very positive results.

(x) **Headaches** : Lemon tea relieves headache (It is prepared by replacing milk with a few drops of lemon juice).

(xi) **Nausea, vomitting and Travel sickness** : Having a glassful of lemon juice diluted a bit with water ensure your not suffering from any sort of the above mentioned sickness.

(xii) **Sun-stroke or heat-stroke** : Lemon or lime (*musambi*) juice prevents sun stroke or heat stroke. Before going out in the harsh sun have a glassful of cool *Shikanjavi* to avoid all disorders by heat.

(xiii) **Whooping Cough** : Lemon or *Musambi* (lime) is an age-old house hole remedy for this trouble.

(xiv) **Low Vitality** : People suffering from this problem should have lemon-honey mixed water for immediate cure. Replace honey with sugar candy (*misri*) if honey be not available.

(xv) **Lemon juice as beautifier** : Lemon has been an old remedy to cure skin blemishes and a beautifying agent. Rubbing your face with the peel of lemon after 10 mts. of your having applied a little of fresh cream is an ideal astringent to bring back your youthful looks. It removes all the blemishes and wrinkles. While applying either fresh cream or rubbing it off with the lemon peel make sure that your strokes are far away from the nose. In short, they should be in the opposite direction you feel your wrinkles are forming in. Adding a few drops of lemon juice to the water you take bath which keeps your skin glowing.

4. GINGER THERAPY

Called *Zingiber Officinale*, ginger is a perennial plant widely cultivated in Asia for its aromatic, pungent rhizome (underground stem) used as a spice, flavouring food and medicine. Its use in India and China has been known from ancient times and by the first century AD traders had taken ginger to the Mediteranean region.

The spice has a pleasant, slightly biting taste, and is usually dried and ground to flavour breads, sauces, curry dishes, confectionaries, pickles and ginger ale. The fresh rhizome is used in cooking. The peeled rhizomes may be preserved by boiling in syrup. It acts as digestive, carminative, stomachic, anti-pyreutic, generates heat, expels flatus and cough, purifies blood and is invigorating. It is recommended in atonic dyspepsia, chronic bronchial cough and palpitation of heart. It is corrective to nauseous medicines and analgesic. It checks griping due to purgative and is needed as flavouring agent.

GINGER AS THE CURE OF AILMENTS

(i) **Cold Cōugh and Asthma**

Take 1 tsp mixture of ginger juice, garlic juice, honey and lick two to three limes a day to get relief from bronchial congestion.

Prepare the pill in the following way: take 10 gms. each of dry ginger (*saunth*), black ginger and 100 gms. jaggery (old) and grind them to a paste form and then make pea-sized pills. Suck this pill 4 to 6 times every day to get relief in chest and stomach congestion due to excess of phelgm in the body.

Heated ginger juice with honey (1 tsp) each 3 times a day for few days to get cure from cough and relief in Asthma.

10 gms. of ginger pieces boiled in water and taken with sugar and diluted tea cures cold and cough.

(ii) **Digestive Problems**

Taking 2 tsp of juice of ginger, fresh lemon and honey in equal quantity early in the morning helps in digestion, increases appetite and improves blood circulation.

6 gms. of ginger pieces with sendha namak taken before meals for 10 days relieves flatulence.

Powder of dry ginger, asatfoetida and sendha namak taken after meals quickly relieves flatulence.

Having small pieces of fresh ginger fried in pure ghee with little salt twice a day cures digestion. Taking 1 tsp. 'Churna' ([finely powdered *saunth* or dry ginger, *ajwain* and black pepper (10 gms. each)]. Keep green cardamom (*chhoti ilaichee*), sugar candy (5 gms.) finely powdered and preserved in a bottle. Taking little of it after meals cures most of the stomach and digestive problems caused by gas.

Prepare decoction by boiling pieces of ginger, Dhania seeds, little of cumin seeds, 8-10 kismis (raisins) in 150 ml water till it is reduced to half of its original quality. Now strain the potion with the addition of sugar candy. This is especially potent to cure problems related to biliousness.

Drinking milk with pieces of ginger boiled in it eliminates intestinal problem.

(iii) **Diarrhoea and water based disorders**

Taking a few pieces of ginger boiled in water and drinking this water with munching the ginger pieces cures the problem of loose motions.

No matter how severe is the problem of hiccoughs disturbing you, just chew a few bits of fresh ginger and you would get relief immediately.

(iv) **Hoarseness and voice problems**

Taking half teaspoonful ginger juice with honey 3 to 4 times a day cures hoarseness of throat. Another very efficacious treatment is the following. Make a hole in ginger and fill it with little heenga (asafoetida). Wrap this in a cloth and heat it. After grinding it make a small ball like peas and take this tablet 4 to 5 times a day. It cures hoarseness of throat quickly.

(v) **Influenza**

Make the decoction in the following way. Take 3 gms. of dry ginger, 7 Tulsi leaves, 7 black pepper seeds boiled in 250 gms. water with sugar to take. Taking this fluid a few times a day cures cold, cough, headache and brings quick relief in influenza cases. To get relief in case of accumulated sputum, take half tsp of dried *saunth* with a little of *sendha namak* three or four times a week. To cure ribs' pain take dry ginger's decoction obtained by boiling 20 gms. of *saunth* in ½ kg. of water and drink it 3 to 4 times a day.

(vi) **Back-ache due to menstrual disorder**

Prepare the *churna* the following way. Take 1 gm. of powdered *saunth* (dry ginger), 1.5 gms. of edible soda with 2 gms. salt heated on tawa and make 4 doses of the preparation. Have it with hot milk or water before retiring for the day. Alternatively, taking decoction of powdered saunth with old ghee cures backache and regulates menstrual disorders.

(vii) **Arthrities and the gout problem**

Taking 10 gms of saunth boiled in 100 gms. of water with jaggery for sometimes gives great relief in Arthritis troubles. Also munching fresh ginger with a piece of jaggery as and when one may like relieves the stiffness inthe joints.

(viii) **In the cases of parasis and paralysis**
Make the ladoos in the following way: Fry paste of ground urad dal, mix saunth and jaggary (125 gms., 5 gms. and 10 gms. respectively). Eating one laddo every day in the morning helps in curing paralysis.

(ix) **Numbness of the Limbs**
Applying paste of dry ginger and garlic (mixed with water) on the affected parts cures numbness.

Chewing little of dry ginger with two shellots of garlic early in the morning for 10-15 days improves blood circulation and removes numbness of the limbs.

Note : In case you find ginger causing extra heat in the body taking a little of honey or almond oil sets the inbalance in order.

5. PAPAYA THERAPY

Botanically called *Carica Papaya*, the fruit of papaya contains A, B, C Vitamins besides 89.6% water, 9.5% carbohydrates 5% proteins, 1% other extract, mineral salts 4%, calcium 0.1%, phosphorus 2%. Its pulp also has malic, tartaric and citric acid, resins, peper and sugar. The fruit is a rich source of vitamins. 100 gms. pulp has 3000 I. U. Vitamin A, 130 mg-vitamin C and 56 calories. The milk of 'Papita tree' is very rich in 'Pepsin'—a digestive enzyme very useful as medicine. All other parts of Papita tree and fruit also have it.

PAPAYA'S CURATIVE PROPERTIES AND THEIR EFFECT ON VARIOUS ILLNESSES AND DISORDERS

(i) **Indigestion and allied stomach problems**
Taking ripe papita in breakfast eliminates indigestion, flatulence, acidity and enhances appetite. Taking water in which powdered dried leaves are soaked overnight is also useful to set right your digestive disorders.

In case of diarrhoea taking boiled raw Papita cures chronic diarrhoea.

(ii) **Skin troubles**
Applying fresh juice of raw Papita on the affected part cures the skin troubles like eczema, ring worm and itching.

(iii) **Papaya as the beautifying agent**
Applying pulp of ripe Papaya as semi-liquid lotion (*ubtan*) on the affected part at least half an hour before bath eliminates freckles and other blemishes of skin and imparts natural glow and lustre. Applying fresh juice of Papaya is also useful for getting rid of pimples. During the treatment also have at least 250 gms. of Papita everyday in the afternoon.

Massaging pulp of Papaya on the head 10 mts. before shampooing the hair eliminates dandruff.

(iv) **Tonsilitis**
Gargling with water in which little juice of Papita is mixed cures the trouble.

(v) **Lactating problem**
Taking ripe Papita daily helps in getting sufficient milk for the child. During the treatment also eat vegetable cooked with raw Papaya.

(vi) **Menstrual problems**
Taking ripe Papaya daily regulates menses. Also, taking few seeds (powdered) of Papaya with water also helps cure the trouble.

(vii) **High Blood Pressure**
Taking ripe Papaya half an hour before breakfast controls the porblem of hypertension.

(viii) **Infantile troubles**
Taking 10 to 12 drops of raw Papaya controls enlargement of liver and spleen of children.

Swallowing ½ tsp ground, dried seeds of Papaya with water and little salt two times a day is also useful to check the liver and spleen troubles of children.

In the cases of jaundice taking 10-12 drops of raw Papaya juice on 1 *batasha* (little fluffy toffees made from sugar-candy) for 10 to 15 days helps in curing jaundice. Along with it have Papaya in the morning every day.

(ix) **Constipatory Problems**
In cases of stranguary, taking Papaya regularly eliminates all such problems in induces frequent urination.

Have Papaya in the afternoons to keep away from constipation and piles. In cases of fistula applying raw juice on the wound helps in healing.

Worms are also the end result of chronic constipation. In such cases taking ½ tsp. ground seeds of Papita with water for 3 to 4 days helps in clearing worms and also the constipatory tendency.

6. KARELA THERAPY

Botanically called *Hairy Mordica*, Karela or bitter gourd is very bitter in taste. But it is a rich source of phosphorus, so much so, that one Karela a day takes care of the entire need of phosphorus by our body. It is a blood purifier and activates spleen, liver and highly beneficial in diabetes. It is purgative, appetiser, digestive, anti-inflammatory, anti-flatulent and has healing capacity.

It has 92.4% water, 8% minerals, 1.6% proteins, 4.2% fats, 4.2% carbohydrates, 0.03 calcium and 0.07 phosphorus. 100 gms of Karela contain 22mg of iron, 210 (IU) Vitamin A, 24 (IU) Vitamin B and 88 mg Vitamin C.

Karela is useful in curing the following diseases :

(i) **Arthritis**

Massage the affected portion with juice of Karela and eat Karela vegetable to cure pain in joints.

(ii) **Diabetes**

Juice of Karela 5 to 10 gms taken with or without water 3 times a day for 2-3 months eliminates the sugar problem in body. Alternatively or alongwith this treatment taking 3 to 6 gms. of ground karela (cut into pieces, dried in shade and then ground) and washing down with fresh water is also very useful. Also have Karela vegetable a plenty.

(iii) **Leucorrhoea**

Take ½ tsp Karela juice 2 times a day for about two weeks cures this problem.

(iv) **Jaundice**

One to two teaspoonful fresh Karela juice followed by a glass of water cures the malady. However, stop the treatment when yellowness in the eyes disappears.

(v) **Liver trouble (of children)**

Giving half tsp of Karela juice to a child (3 to 8 yrs.) is a good preventive measure to keep the child free of the liver troubles.

(vi) **Worms**

Giving 1 tsp of Karela juice mixed with half teaspoonful of Garlic juice destroys worms and also cures constipation.

(vii) **Piles**

Having 1 tsp of Karela juice with sugar—2 times a day stops oozing of the blood from anus and heals the wound.

(viii) **Constipation**

Taking 5 to 10 drops of the homeopathic medicine '*Memoradica Charantia*' (made from Karela)—4 times a day cures constipation.

(viii) **Blood Purifier**

1-2 tsp of Karela juice in the morning taken for a few days purifies blood and it is also a good cure for pimples.

Normally Karela is a heat-inducing agent, so it shouldn't be taken in the excessive quantity. In case one takes a large dose of Karela juice, taking curd or lemon over it sets right the imbalance.

CHAPTER VII

THE YOGA THERAPY, HUMAN BODY AND THE CURE OF DISEASES

Yoga is the best discipline to keep one mentally and physically healthy. Therapeutic Yoga is basically a system of self-treatment. According to Yogic view, diseases, disorders and ailments are the result of faulty ways of living, bad habits, lack of proper knowledge of things related to individual's life, and improper food. The diseases are thus the resultant state of a short or prolonged malfunctioning of the body system. The malfunctioning is caused by an imbalanced internal condition created due to certain errors committed by the individuals. Since the root cause of a disease lies in the mistakes of the individual, its cure also lies in correcting those mistakes by the same individual. Thus, it is the individual himself who is responsible in both the cases, that is, for causing as well as curing the diseases.

Since this being the basic assumption in this system about the nature of the trouble and its remedy, there is total reliance on the effort of the patient himself. The Yoga expert shows only the path and works no more than as a counsellor to the patient.

Although, Yoga covers all the aspects of one's personality and the things that go to make this world, yet for the purpose of therapy three things are essential (i) Proper diet, (ii) Proper Yoga practice, and (iii) Proper awareness of the world around. If one sticks to these basic principles, one is not likely to have ill-health.

A. HEALTH

A word about health. Good health or fitness is a vague term as far as physiological condition is concerned. What exactly is meant by good health? It means that all the organs of the body must be working in their prime condition. But health includes physical and mental sense of well being. All of us know the oft-repeated proverb, *"If health is lost everything is lost"*. In fact, we realise the importance of a thing or state more by its absence than by its presence. There are many things in our life of which we are hardly aware when they are there, but the moment they are gone we become acutely aware of them. Health is one such thing. When it is there we do not remember it always although it expresses in everything that we do. The importance of the saying *"health is wealth"*, is felt more when health is impaired. The importance of health in life can hardly be overemphasised. To have a healthy body and mind is an asset perhaps more important than having even good education, living in a good house, etc. Happiness is said to be more intimately related to good health (mental and physical both) than to these outside factors. In the wake of all happiness if health is lacking then happiness will certainly be a far cry. It is hardly enough to know that health has great importance. All of us know this fact. What is perhaps more important to know is what are the essential conditions to be fulfilled for being a healthy individual.

Among the factors that influence health we must distinguish between external factors and the internal ones. Environmental conditions, heredity, pattern of behaviour or way of life, work and rest, food habits, cleanliness and exercise may be mentioned. Some of these external factors that go to decide whether an individual will be healthy or otherwise. We shall not discuss these factors. First we would like our discerning readers to know about the body components or body systems whose efficient functioning defines good health.

There are seven basic systems of the human body : (i) Digestive system (ii) Excretory System (iii) The Respiratory System (iv) The Circulatory System (v) Muscular System (vi) The Skeletal System (vii) The Nervous System. We shall discuss these one by one.

(i) **Digestive System** : The food that we take comprises proteins, sugars and starches, vitamins, salts, fats and oils. Only a part of these substances is useful to the body and the rest, which is indigestible, must be got rid of. The food is broken up by the teeth and after getting mixed with saliva, is swallowed. Saliva is an alkaline fluid which is poured into the mouth from salivary glands. Digestion of food starts in the mouth itself. From the mouth the food enters an expanded cavity behind, the Pharynx, which is also common to the air passage at this level. It then passes into the gullet. Like stomach and intestines, the gullet is a muscular organ and can force the food along if necessary. With the help of the muscle, a man can drink even if he is standing on his head. About nine inches long, the gullet ends in the stomach. It is here that the second stage of digestion takes place.

From this position the food reaches stomach which is a hollow muscular organ lined by a glandular mucus membrane which secretes the gastric juice. Gastric juice is made up of hydrochloric acid, salts, pepsin and water. The stomach mixes the food well by moving it round and round. At this stage the proteins are changed to a form in which they can pass through the stomach wall and be absorbed, at once ready to nourish the body. Starches and proteins are now acted upon, though not digested completely. Fat and oil are broken up and the oil is set free. In the stomach, digestion may take two to three hours. The food then goes to small intestine which is a long tube which, when uncoiled, may measure about 1 feet. Here, we have to consider the action of three different digestive juices, e.g., the pancreatic juice, the bile generated by the liver and the intestinal juice, which is the secretion of the small glands of the bowel lining. Food passes through the wall of the intestine into the lacteal, and so into the blood. The bile and the pancreatic juice are produces by the liver and pancreas respectively.

Liver is the largest organ in the body, which is situated just underneath the diaphragm rather on the right side. Its weight is three to four pounds. There are fine tubes in the liver called bile ducts into which the cells of the liver secrete bile, and the bile ducts join together and form Hepatic duct which carries the bile to the duodenum (also known as first part of small intestine).

Bile is a yellow fluid, containing mucus, water and especial salts (called bile salts). It acts on the fats and oils and breaks them up into very small drops. Liver is also a storehouse for sugar which it puts in the blood, when it is required by the body. About seven inches long, there is another large gland reddish in colour and known as Pancreas. It lie behind the stomach, and a tube from it called the Pancreatic duct enters the intestine near where the bile duct enters. The pancreatic juices act on the protein, the starches and the fats.

The intestine is an organ of digestion as well as of absorption. The food, now digested, can pass through the walls of the intestine and is taken into the blood. It is then distributed all over the body. Food remains in the small intestine for about 12 hours and is slowly passed on towards the large intestine.

The large intestine is a 6 feet long tube. It is little concerned with digestion or absorption of food, for more of this has already been done. Food remains here from 24 to 36 hours. Due to loss of water, the material in the large intestine now hardens as it reaches the rectum. Finally, the indigestible remnant is turned out.

(ii) **The Excretory System** : Termed as the *'Sanitary System'* of the *'City of Body'*, it comprises the kidney, skin, lungs and bowels. The system is designed to help get rid of the waste matter in the body when all juices have been extracted from the digestive food. There are two kidneys, situated one on each side of the backbone in the small of the back or loin. It has the renal artery which brings blood to it, and the renal vein which takes it away. In addition, there are the usual nerves, the lymphatic vessels and the Ureter, the tube that takes urine from the kidney to the bladder. The bladder is the reservoir for urine.

Urine, a pale yellow fluid, carrying the waste nitrogen from our protein foods and also mineral salts, is secreted into the two kidneys. The kidney may be regarded as a pair of filters, through which about 2 pints of blood circulates every minute. In fact, the whole blood in the body passes down to the kidneys in five to six minutes. Urine is propelled down along the ureters from the kidneys to the bladder by successive veins of contraction in the muscular walls of these channels.

The bladder is an elastic membrane serving as a temporary reservoir for urine, secreted by the kidneys. The normal adult capacity is about 1 pint. The urine is discharged into the bladder in intermittent jets every 20 seconds or so. The outlet below the bladder is normally closed by a tight ring of muscle called Sphincter. In emptying, the bladder contracts and the sphincter relaxes to allow efflux of urine.

Another important agent for excretion of the waste material from the body is skin. It has two layers, the top one called the Epidermis or scarf skin and dermis or true skin. The latter is richly supplied with blood vessels. The skin is designed to :
  (a) protect the body ;
  (b) act as an organ of excretion by means of sweat glands. It thus helps to regulate the temperature of the body ; and
  (c) to give the sense of touch.

The skin has hair and sense organs. The latter are little lumps in the dermis which are nerve ending. They report to the nervous system when anything comes into their contact. The skin also has two kinds of glands, the Sebaceous glands, which secrete an oily substance serving as lubricant to the skin and the Sweat glands which make the skin as an excretory organ. The function of the latter is to take up sweat from the blood and pour it out on the skin. Though mostly water, the sweat contains salts, fats and tiny bits of skin.

Bowels are the intestines, both large and small which serve to complete the digestion of food and to allow of its absorption into the blood-stream. The useless food remains are gradually moved onwards and are hardened in the large intestine wherefrom they are ready to be thrown out. The failure of the bowel function is called constipation.

Lumps comprise two elastic spongy masses, almost filling the chest cavity. These are import agents to cleanse the system of impurity. Lungs throw off carbon dioxide, water (in the shape of vapour) and also some organic matter. They are, therefore, organs of excretion in addition to being organs of respiration.

(iii) **The Respiratory System** : This system comprises the lungs and the passages leading to them.

Respiratory System

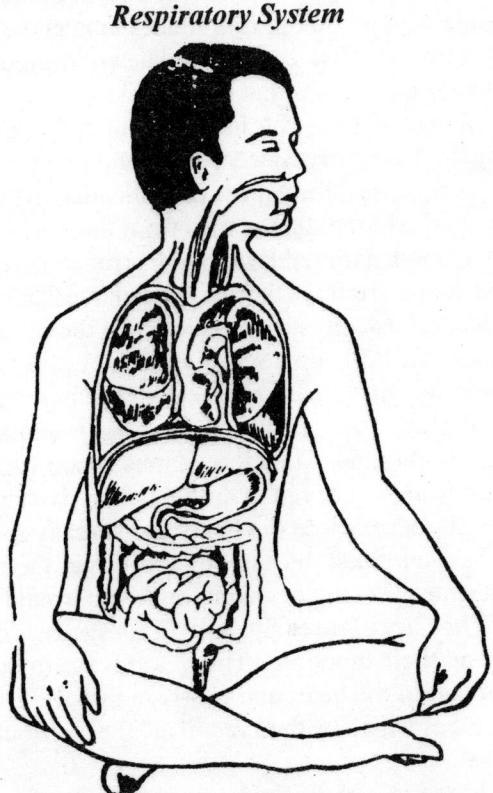

The purpose of respiration (breathing) is the entry and exit of air to and from the lungs. In in-breathing (or inspiration or inhalation) the chest cavity is enlarged and the air enters, in out-breathing (expiration)

the chest cavity reverses its action and the air is thrown out. The object of breathing is to bring oxygen of the air into contact with the blood with the purpose of (a) giving some oxygen to the blood, and (b) taking of waste products from the blood.

The air, in going to the lungs, has to go through various passages. They are nose or mouth, and the larynx or voice box.

We breathe through nose or through mouth. These are two passages leading downwards from nose and mouth into the body one takes food and water to the stomach and the other takes air to the lungs.

Larynx or Voice box is commonly known as *"Adam's Apple"* and can easily be felt in the throat. It is a cavity (in throat) holding vocal cords, just at its function with pharynx. Vibration of cords produces vocal sounds. The air passes from the voice box to the lungs by means of wind-pipe which is about four inches long and one inch wide. It has rings of gristles which keep it open. The wind-pipe at the lower end, is divided into two branches that go to the lungs.

The functioning of the lungs has already been described while discussing the Excretory System. Here the functioning of lungs as the respiratory organ is slightly more complicated. In the lungs, the air gets very close to the blood, that comes from the muscles by way of heart. The impure blood, dark red in colour, has too much carbon dioxide in it. This blood comes from the tissues which have taken the oxygen from it but have loaded it with carbon dioxide. In the tissues, oxygen is used every minute to burn up food material, resulting in production of considerable quantity of carbon dioxide. The lung's function is to reverse this state of affairs, i.e., restoring its oxygen quota and expelling the excess carbon dioxide. Thus the venous blood (the impure blood) is rendered arterial (bright red in colour) in its passage through the lung capillaries. It goes back to the heart and is ready to do its work again. The new oxygen, taken by the blood all over the body, is picked up again by its muscles which need it for their normal functioning.

(iv) **The Circulatory System** : This system comprises the blood and heart and their functions. The blood is continuously propelled by the contraction of the heart and is driven into the arteries. The arteries are elastic tubes which by their recoil aid the distribution of the blood to all parts.

The blood is a clear fluid comprising innumerable solid bodies called corpuscles. The corpuscles are of two kinds, red and white and are cellular shaped. The red corpuscles carry Haemoglobin which constitutes protein and a little iron. When combined with oxygen, haemoglobin forms a bright red substance and with carbon dioxide it forms a blush compound. The white corpuscles are living organism, small jelly-like creatures each with a nucleus. They are of great importance as they eat up the disease germs that enter the body. They are capable of independent movement in the blood stream and within the tissue, and can swallow up dead bacteria and foreign particles.

The main function of blood are the following :
(a) It carries oxygen to every part of the body that requires it.
(b) It carries impurities from all parts of the body to the excretory organs namely the lungs, the kidneys and the skin.
(c) It carries food from the digestive system to all tissues.
(d) It carries heat to all parts of the body.

The heart is a hollow, muscular and somewhat conical four chambered force pump enclosed in a fibrous bag. It is situated in the chest between the lungs and weighs from 10 to 12 ounces. The heart is divided into two parts by a wall running from top to bottom with no direct connection between the parts. These parts are themselves divided into parts, upper and lower but have valves between them. The upper portions are called Auricles and the lower one Ventricles.

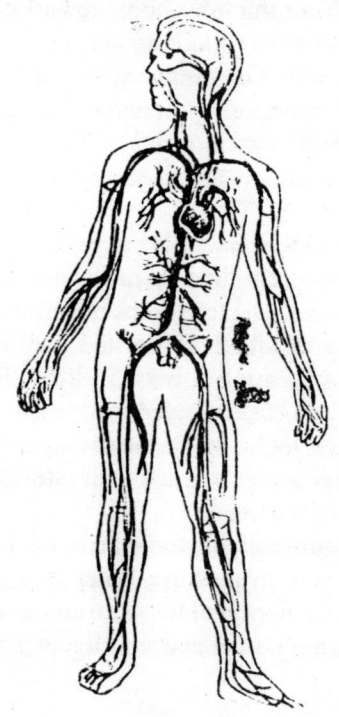

The motive power of the circulation is the pumping action of the heart which acts as boosting mechanism set in the middle of a pipeline. When the blood reaches the tissues it loses all its oxygen and is loaded with waste material from the tissues. The impure blood reaches the heart by means of capillaries and veins. With the beat of the heart, it enters into the Right Auricle and then to the Right Ventricle from where it is taken by the Pulmonary Artery to the lungs. In the lung capillaries, the blood comes into contact with oxygen and is purified. The purified blood is now brought back to heart by means of Pulmonary Vein. It now enters the left Auricle and when auricles are squeezed during the heart-beat, the blood passes to the left Ventricle and then commences its journey again to all parts of the body. Thus with the contraction of right and left auricles, the venous blood from the body and aerated blood from the lungs is pumped into their respective ventricles. And when the right and left ventricles contract, venous blood is pumped into the lungs and the aerated blood into the main vessels. These rhythmic contractions and dilations, followed by an equivalent pause are called pulse or heart beat.

(v) **Muscular System** : Muscles are attached to the bones and consist of bundles of fleshly fibres, capable of contraction or shortening when required. Such contractions help the various limbs of the body to move. The muscles are of two kinds namely the voluntary muscles whose movements are controlled by human will and the involuntary muscles which perform their function without any conscious effort of the will. These include the heart, the muscles of the stomach and those of the intestines. Their movements are rhythmic and we are not conscious of their action.

(vi) **The Skeletal System** : The bony skeleton supporting the human body is constructed to strengthen the muscles which produce movement in the body to give shape. The fore limbs of the human body are supported by bones forming a shoulder girdle and similarly the leg bones are connected to others forming a pelvic girdle. Ribs connected to the backbone (including those connected to the breast bone) serve to protect certain internal organs, including the heart and the lungs. Man's structural superiority over other animals is due to the straight femur or thigh bone and his erect poise of the head.

The above features enable the man to walk in an erect position so that his hands are free to perform other functions. These structural advantages and the formation of his skull and lower jaw are responsible for an increase in brain power and intelligence in man, compared with the other animals.

The human system consists of 206 bones of various sizes. The bones are composed of cells, which are softer in early childhood than in adult life. Where bones meet there is a joint, which may simply be an immovable function as in the bones of the skull or may be movable joint as that of the knee. The movable joints are necessary for the motion of human body.

(vii) **The Nervous System** : It is the most important system since it commands rest of the body what to do and how to work together. While the central nervous system resides in the skull and the spine, the nerves are spread all over the body. The nervous system of man is a network pervading the whole body, having a two-way connection with the central control and enabling the individual to give a coordinated response to any stimulus from outside. Thus nerves that carry the messages to the muscles with orders to perform a particular action are called Motor Nerves.

The brain is the chief centre of the nervous system and is contained within the skull. The brain substance consists of grey and white matter, the grey matter forming a thin, superficial layer (cortex). It consists of three parts: (a) the cerebrum or bigger brain, which govern our consciousness, thought, emotions, will, sight, hearing, sensation of pain and memory through the grey matter, (b) the cerebellum or the smaller brain is connected with the coordination of the actions, nervous and muscular, by which the movement of the body are carried on, (c) the Medulla Oblongata houses the centres of nervous tissue connected with reflex action consisting of movements that take place automatically, such as breathing or walking.

The spinal cord consist mostly of nerves. This is like a continuation of the medulla and runs down the back, surrounded by the bony arch of the spinal column. This organ is capable of making simple decisions, called the reflex action.

THE ENDOCRINE GLANDS

The endocrine glands or ductless glands are situated in the different parts of the body. The thyroid in the neck, the pineal and pituitary in the brain and the adrenals above the kidneys. The ovaries in women and testes in men are situated respectively in pelvis and scrotum. These glands secrete both externally and internally. These secretions play vital role in our nervous system by striking a physiological balance. If these secretions suffer in quantity and quality, it leads to various physical and mental disturbances. For example the inadequate thyroid secretion may result in degeneration of arteries, mental weakness, wrinkles on faces etc. The growth and activity of cells, the ultimate unit of our body, is coordinated by harmones released into the blood stream by various ductless glands.

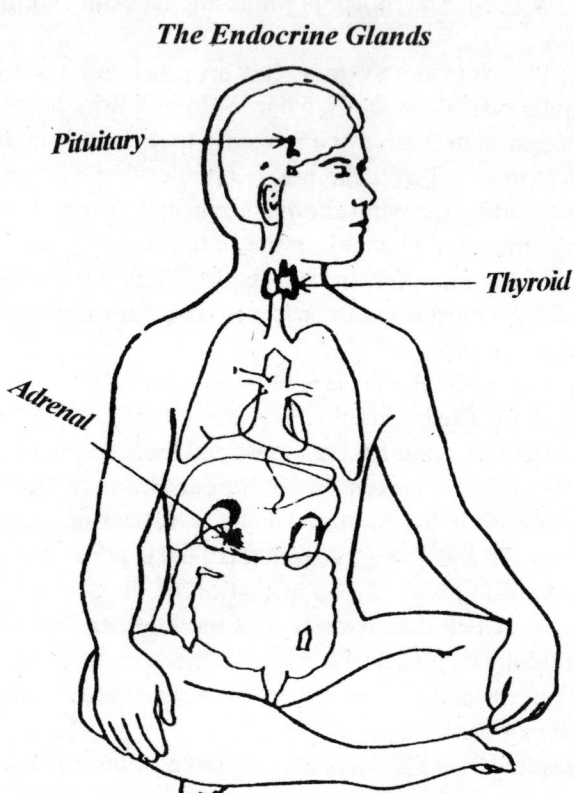

The Endocrine Glands

THE BENEFITS TO THE HUMAN SYSTEM BY YOGIC EXERCISES

As is clear from the above discussion that these different body systems provide cells with nutrition and repair their wear and tear. This combined process is called metabolism. Our body is made up of millions and millions of cells. They need constant nourishment and repair. This harmony is what is referred to as good health. Underuse and understimulation of our vital organs cause so many diseases and poor or ill-health. The regular Yoga practice prevent these. Yoga exercise is unique in the sense that it aims not at developing muscles but at toning up the whole body system so as to affect proper blood circulation, nourishment of tissues and cells, removal of waste product and restoration of metabolism. Regular practice of Yoga keeps the muscles healthy, joints and spine supple, strong and flexible by the combination of various forward, backward and sideways movements. Deep abdominal breathing and pranayam make lungs elastic and healthy, increase their intaking capacity and also keep the air passage clear. The vertical Asanas direct our blood circulation towards the thyroid, resulting in massage and stimulation. The pituitary is the centre of sympathetic nervous system and it also regulates the secretion of all other glands. The Asana like Sheershasana stimulates the pituitary glands, thereby providing proper balance between the body and the gland. Thus the intellectual and physical part of the brain become refreshed by this exercise. The Asanas and other Bandha and Kriyas stinulate the body system and provide us perennial state of good health.

B. THE YOGIC KRIYAS AND BANDHAS

These Yogic Kriyas and Bandhas are the purification processes of the body by Yogic methods.

Kriyas are to be practised early in the morning before sun rise, on empty stomach. Kriyas must be finished before starting the Asanas or Pranayams.

The Kriyas consist of six purification practices (i) Neti (ii) Dhauti (iii) Basti (iv) Kapalbhati (v) Naul (vi) Tratak.
  (i) Neti : It is two types—Jala Neti and Sutra Neti.
      (a) Jala Neti : For doing this, squat on your feet. Take tepid salted water in a medium sized pot with a long spout, made especially for this purpose.

Now fill the pot with tepid salted water and hold it in your right hand to the level of your nose. Then till your head slightly to the left so as to have the slanting position of the left nostril. Insert the nozzle of the spout into the right nostril and allow the water to flow down slowly. The water should continue falling down from the other nostril in a continuous thin stream. Now repeat the process from the other side. Breathe through the mouth only till the Kriya is complete. After Jala neti, stand erect with your feet togethger. Keep the hands behind your back, clapsed and blow out vigorously whatever trace of water that has remained in your nostrils.

Jala Neti

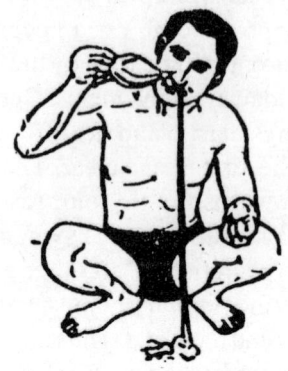

(b) **Sutra Neti** : Sutra Neti is performed with a 12 inch long piece of waxed cord. It is partly twisted and it makes the nasal insertion possible.

Squat on your feet. Take tepid salted water and soak the Neti well in it. Now take the waxed and twisted end of the cord and make it into a curve. Bend your head slightly forward and insert the end of the cord into the nostril through which you have been breathing at that time. Push the cord gradually through the nose, down the throat. Now open your mouth wide, put your index and middle fingers in and with their tips catch the inside end of the cord and draw it out.

Sutra Neti

Hold both the ends in your hand separately and pull the cord very gently up and down 3 to 4 times. Then take it out, wash it and then repeat the cycle with the other nostril.

After completion of the Kriya, wash the cord with soap well and leave it to dry in some clean and safe place. Make sure that the flies, etc., don't pollute it.

(ii) **Dhauti (Vastra)** : Vastra, Dhauti cleans the digestive tract right from the mouth to the stomach. This Kriya or process involve swallowing up of a strip about 20 feet long and 2-3 inches wide. This strip is made of fine spotless white cloth. The strip is first sterilized in boiling water and is then swallowed inch by inch by chewing it. In the beginning only an inch or two may be swallowed but by swallowing a few more inches every day, finally one may learn to swallow it the full. Then it is pulled out slowly and gently. Thus it removes the mucous and other wastes accumulated in the food tube and the stomach. But it should not be practised unless there is some expert to demonstrate and then to guide and supervise the whole process. It may by practised once or twice a week.

(iii) **Basti** : Basti flushes the colour clean. The process of Basti is quite elaborate and complicated and should be done under expert guidance only. This Kriya like an enema involves sucking up the water into bowels with a tube inserted in the rectum. Then this drawn up water is churned in the colon by the process of Uddiyan Bandh and Nauli Kriya and then passed out through the rectum.

(iv) **Kapalbhati** : Kapal means skill and Bhati means shine or lusture. Thus this term literally means skull shining. Kapalbhati is a pranayam also besides one of the six cleaning exercises. Actually this Kriya or cleansing process is a milder form of Bhastrika, another vigorously breathing exercise.

Persons with High Blood Pressure problems or pus in the ear should refrain from the doing this exercise.

We are not giving its elaborate technique, lest it may confuse the reader. We request the reader to learn it from an expert in Yogic Kriyas. We are now giving only its benefits.

Benefits : This Kapalbhati, or Dhauti are very good, invigorating exercise which cleanses the entire respiratory system by forcefully rushing exhalation. It improves concentration and mental retention. The movement of the diaphragm stimulates the stomach, heart, liver and spleen. This exercise is very good for eyes.

(v) **Nauli** : It is the best exercise for preserving and promoting the health of abdominal viscera.

Nauti is equal to Uddiyana Bandh. Nauli should be practised daily in the morning on empty stomach and evacuated bowels.

Method : Stand with legs one foot apart. Bend the legs a little and stoop forward.

Rest the palms on thighs just above your knees, with fingers spread. Press the thighs well with your palms and the chest with your chin at the notch between the collar bones.

Inhale deeply then exhale vigorously so as to force out all the air from the lungs.

Suspend the breath and pull the abdominal region back towards the spine so that a hollow is formed.

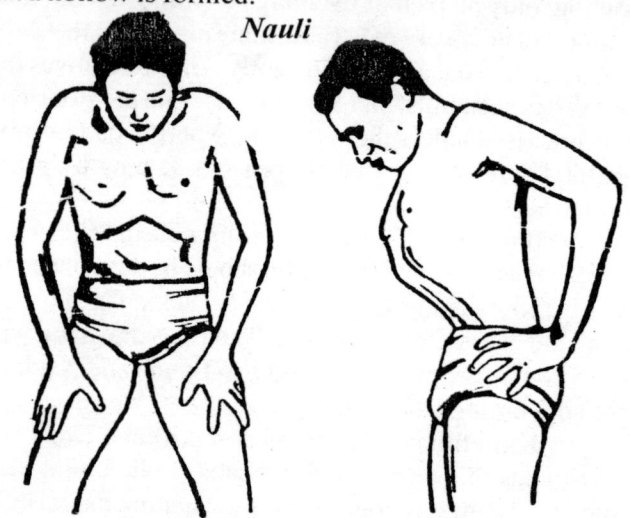

Nauli

Push the abdominal recti forward so that a vertical ridge down the centre is formed. Remain in this position for a few seconds and then relax the grip and inhale smoothly.

Breathe deeply 3-4 times and then repeat the cycle. Repeat it 5-7 times.

Benefits : The benefits of nauli are many. It strengthens abdominal muscles, stomach, intestines and liver. Women who suffer from menstrual problem get immediate relief. It increases gastric fire and helps eliminating the toxic elements from the digestive system. It also helps remove ovarian insufficiency. Nauli quickly cures constipation, dyspepsia, flatulence, etc.

(vi) **Tratak** : It is an amazing exercise to improve your power of concentration. It can be practised with a burning candle or with a black dot on a piece of paper fixed on the wall. Start this practice indoors as there will be less objects to disturb your concentration.

Sitting on the floor in any comfortable or Padmasana pose, have a few deep breath, then make your breath steady, even and rhythmic. Keep the object of your gaze at your eye level at a distance of 3 to 4 feet. Keep the eyes meditatively wide open.

Now gaze at the object steadily without winking till tears well up in your eyes. Close the eyes to let the tears trickle down.

Tratak

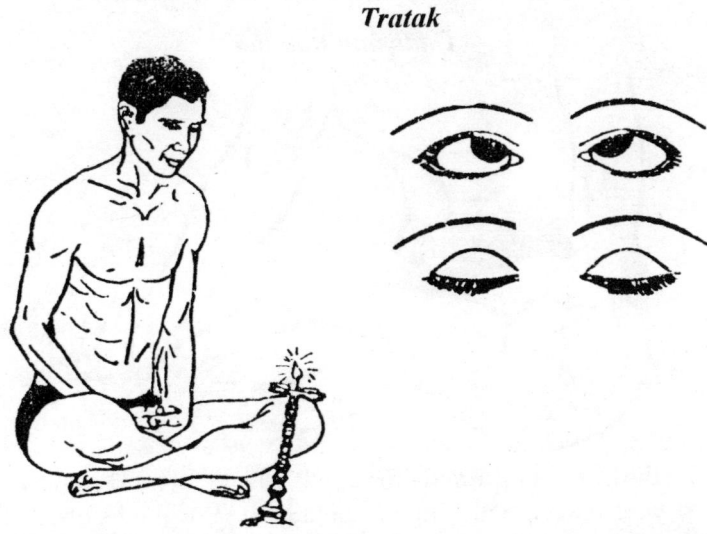

Now mentally visualise that object. When the mental image vanishes, open your eyes and start gazing afresh. Do not strain your nerves and be relaxed. Let not your mind wander. Try to bring your mind back to the object but without straining yourself much as that would sap your energy and you will be tired soon.

After practising with the point on the wall or on a steady flame, try to do it. Concentrating on the tip of your nose or on the point between the eye-brows.

Tratak improves eye sight and removes the disease of your eyes if any. It helps in concentrating your mind and purifies your mind.

Bandhas : Bandhas literally mean a lock, bondage or joining together to objects or stages. A Bandha is a special posture invented to conserve and make greater use of vast resources of energy engerated by yogic exercises and Pranayam. Thus these bandhas are a means of reorientation and control of the vital energy of you body and mind. These are of three main types :

(i) Jalandhar Bandha (ii) Uddiyana Bandha (iii) Mula Bandha.

(i) **Jaladhar Bandha** : In this bandha the throat is contracted and locked, as it were, by making the chin rest on the chest in the notch between the collar bones. In certain Asanas or posture like Sarvangasana exhalation and fresh inhalation when the breath is suspended. Once in a day early in the morning it should be practised, first standing then in advanced stage, in sitting position.

Technique : Stand erect with your feet one foot apart.

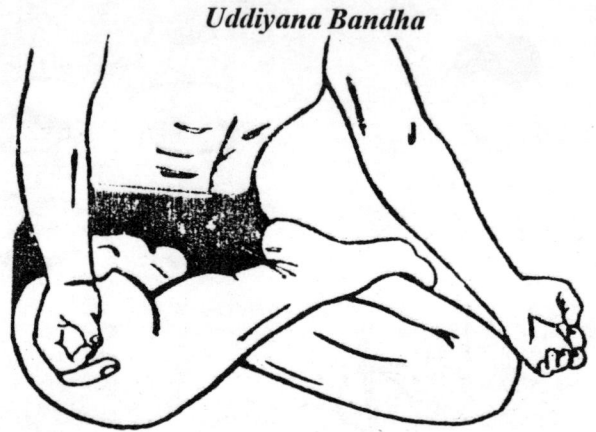

Uddiyana Bandha

Bend the knees a little and then slightly bend forward.

Rest your palms, with fingers spread, on your thighs above the knees.

Take a few deep breaths and then exhale forcefully this is automatically practised. In these postures the chin is firmly pressed against the chest. This chin lock regulates the flow of blood to the heart, head, brain and neck, Jaladhar Bandha is also practised in combination with Mula Bandha.

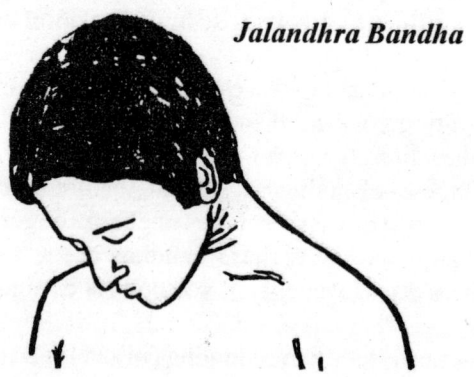

Jalandhra Bandha

(ii) **Uadiyana Bandha** : It is a very powerful bandha and a basic one for regulating the flow of prana and awakening of Kundalini. Uddiyana involves the lifting up of the Diaphragm high up the chest and pulling up the abdominal organs towards the spine. It means to fly up. This bandha makes the great bird of prana fly towards the highest chakra Brahmrandhra or Sahasrara. It is to be practised between the full so as to empty your lungs completely. Press your chin against the chest in chin lock.

Keep the breath suspended and pull the entire abdominal region back towards your spine. Then draw it up towards thorax. Keep the pressure of your palms on the thighs all this time. Remain in the pose for 20-30 seconds according to your capacity.

Relax the grip on your abdominal region and inhale slowly and deeply.

Repeat the cycle 3-5 times.

Effects
1. Uddiyana Bandha is of great spiritual value as it forces the prana up the Sushumna nadi.
2. In invigorates the whole abdominal region.
3. It is said to rejuvenate an old person, if it is properly and constantly practised.
4. The uplifting of diaphragm massages the heart muscles.

(iii) **Mula Bandha** : Mula literally means the root, source, foundation or the basis. In it the portion between anus and scrotum is contracted and raised. This prevents Apana escaping from the lower body and draws it up to unite with Prana.

Technique : Sit in Padmasan or Siddhasan. Stretch your hands and fingers as if in Jnana Mudra. Now inhale deeply and retain your breath. Press the chin against the chest in the chin lock. Now contract the region of lower abdomen between the anus and the navel towards your spine and pull it upwards towards the diaphragm. Than contract and pull towards the abdominal muscles and remain in the posture for a few seconds. Now release the grip on anal sphincter and abdominal muscles and remove the chin lock. Exhale slowly and evenly. Repeat the cycle 3 to 5 times.

Benefits : The benefits of this Bandha are many. It prevents the Apana Vayu (the foul wind) escaping from the lower body and draws it up to unite with the Prana Vayu (the vital wind). It increases sexual retention power which when sublimated makes a man 'Urdhvaretus' or a person of great moral and spiritual power. It also helps in awakening the dorment kundalini (the ultimate power of the body which lay dorment like a coiled snake, hence the name kundalini) by preventing the dissipation of pranic energy and changing it into a spiritual force.

This Mula Bandha should be practised when one becomes quite deft in doing certain difficult. Asanas or postures like Sheershasana, Sarvangasana, etc.

As discussed earlier, these Kriyas and Bandha prepare your body to start your asanas. They purify the body totally so that the absence of any toxic material in the body is fully ensured. Then one should do the asana to derive their full effect. It is not necessary to do all the Bandhas and Kriyas together. First of all, choose any one of them, practise them thoroughly, then do your asanas which have been discussed ahead.

C. THE YOGIC ASANAS OR EXERCISES

Before doing these Yogic Asanas, the following precautions must be taken :

(i) All these Asanas (barring those about which we'd mention while discussing them) must be practised on empty stomach and clean bowels and preferably after bath.

(ii) They should not be practised after taking meals or even breakfast. At least an hour should be allowed to lapse after a very light breakfast in performing these Asanas. Give 3 to 4 hours time to your taking meals. Meals can be taken half an hour after the Yoga session.

(iii) Select a well-ventilated, quiet and clean place to do these Asanas. Never do them in your bed or on uneven surface.

(iv) The best time to practise Asanasis either early in the morning or late in the evening when your are cool, clam, relaxed in mind and not in a hurry and huff.

(v) A carpet, mattress or a folded blanket accommodating the full length and breadth of the person should be used. It may also be covered with a well washed piece of cloth for better comfort.

(vi) The session need not be gone through at a stretch. It should be conveniently punctuated with relaxation poses. Select a few Asanas and do them regularly.

1. PRANAYAAM (BREATH CONTROL)

Pranayaam means control of the motions of exhalation and inhalation.

Method : Let the internal breath be thrown out with force through the nostrils and retained outside according to one's capacity. After having resorted to this external process thrice, let the breath be taken in slowly to retain it there, to be thrown out in gradual process when you experience uneasiness. This internal process should be brought into play repeatedly according to one's will and capacity.

The retained or suspended breath needs to be held up voluntarily at one's will for a while. During this process inhalation the air is kept at day. This practice of holding up the breath is known as 'Stambha-Vriti' which enhances the power of concentration. So long as mastery over breath-control is not feasible or when its attainment causes uneasiness, throw out breath slowly, but let the breath drawn in be suspended midway. In the same way exhalation or inhalation of the air be adhered to according to one's will and capability. This is known "Vahya-Abhyantarak-Shepi" Kriya. All these four processes constitute a full Pranayaam.

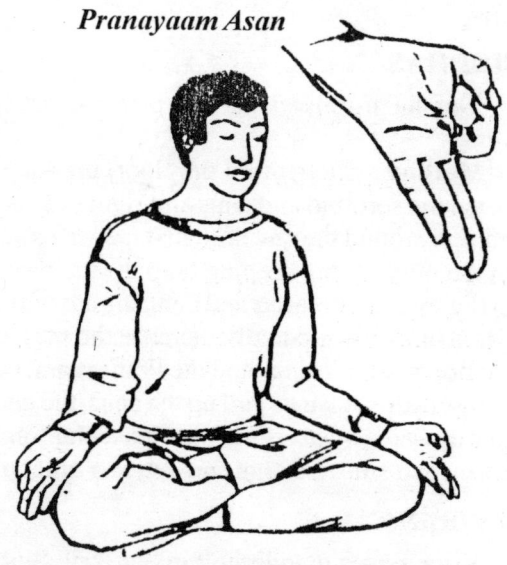

Pranayaam Asan

Benefits: By doing pranayaam regularly, the body gets full rest. The abdomen is purified of the vile fluids and gases and other impurities. The fat of the stomach gets arrested and the chest gets widened. It enhances the power of concentration, the circulation of blood and restores the healthy look of the aging body. This exercise should by done either in the morning or in the evening at a open place.

2. PADMASANA

This Asanas or posture is called Padmasana as the forms of legs while performing this Asanas gives the appearance of Padma (lotus).

Method : While sitting on the ground, stretch your legs forward. Keep them together. Place the right foot on the left thigh and the left foot on the right thigh in such a manner that the heels of both the feet touch the abdomen, on the sides of the navel. Keep the hands on the knees. Keep body, back and head erect. The knees of both the feet should touch ground and generally the eyes should remain closed. One should do Pranayaam also in this pose.

Benefits : This Asanas is highly advantageous for attaining concentration of mind and is very efficacious for those who do mental work, particularly the aged people. It is a unique way of preserving vital fluids of the body and preventing the trapping of the wind inside the body. It imparts peace, solitude and ensures longevity. It also prevents abdominal disease and female disorder connected with the reproductive organs.

3. SIDDHASANA

'Siddha' means adepts who perform the Asanas to derive supernal powers.

Method : Sit erect on the floor, pressing the heel of the left leg between the scrotum and anus and right heel between the genitalia and the region around the navel, so that the knees and the heels, both lie one upon the other. Thus keeping both the hands on either sole of the feet, keep the eyes half closed and concentrate with in. Sit for a convenient duration and then gradually increase the period. After having attained perfection in this Asanas and the Pranayaam, do them regularly. While performing this Asanas, pull up the anus, the genitals and the abdominal organs upwards by exerting intra-muscular force. This Asana should be performed at sun-rise or at sun-set, at a quiet place.

4. VAJRASANA

Vijra means thunderbolt in Sanskrit. Since this Asana makes the body as strong as the thunderbolt, it is so named.

Method : Kneel down on the floor with your knees, ankles and big toes touching the ground. Now sit down on your heels and place your palms on the knees. Keep yourself erect but relaxed. Breath should be deep even and slow. Now expand your chest and draw the abdominal region inwards.

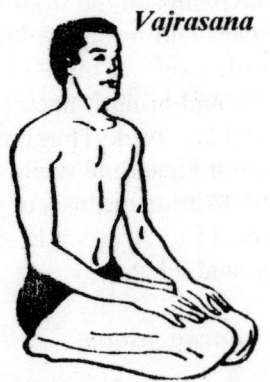
Vajrasana

Benefits : This Asana is especially good for those who suffer from high blood pressure. This posture can be practised any time even after taking meals. It strengthens spine, removes pain in the spine and tones up sexual organs of both male and female. Its regular practice gives longevity and postpones old age.

5. SARVANGASANA

Since this one Asana activates the nerves and muscles of the entire body, it is named so. Sarvang means all parts in Sanskrit.

Method : Lie down on the back and relax completely. Inhale, then while exhaling slowly, raise the legs, hips and trunk in a continuous movement until vertical. Raise the legs—keeping the knees straight and hips by supporting the arms on the ground, then bend the elbows and hold the trunk in the hands. In this posture the chin is baried in the sternum (upper chest). Practise respiration in the portion and retain the position as long as it is comfortable. Direct the attention to the thyroid gland (in the neck). To return to the starting position, gently lower the trunk, pelvis and legs, and relax on the ground. Repeat the exercise two to three times but do it in a comfortable manner. This Asana may appear slightly difficult in the beginning but regular practice can solve this problem. This one posture or Asana is good enough to rejuvenate your whole body systems.

6. BHVJANGASANA

Since Bhujang means a snake, this posture in which the body attains the shape of a raised-hood-stance of a snake, it is named so.

Method : Lie flat on your belly, on the floor. Now place your palms on the floor by the side of your trunk. Keep the elbows bent. Then, exhaling slowly lift the head and trunk-back upwards. Straighten your elbows by pressing the palms on the floor and raising the trunk. The, exhaling, bend the knees and bring the legs in a perpendicular position to the ground. While exerting more pressure on right hand, remove the left off the floor and bring it back to clasp the left knee. Now, similarly bring the right arm back, Thus balanced on your thighs and pelvic region, pull on your knees and while exhaling increase the curve of your spine. Now, try to bring the back of your head and the feet in contact. Hold the pose for 15 to 20 seconds, then release the knees and come down to the floor, and relax.

Savangasana

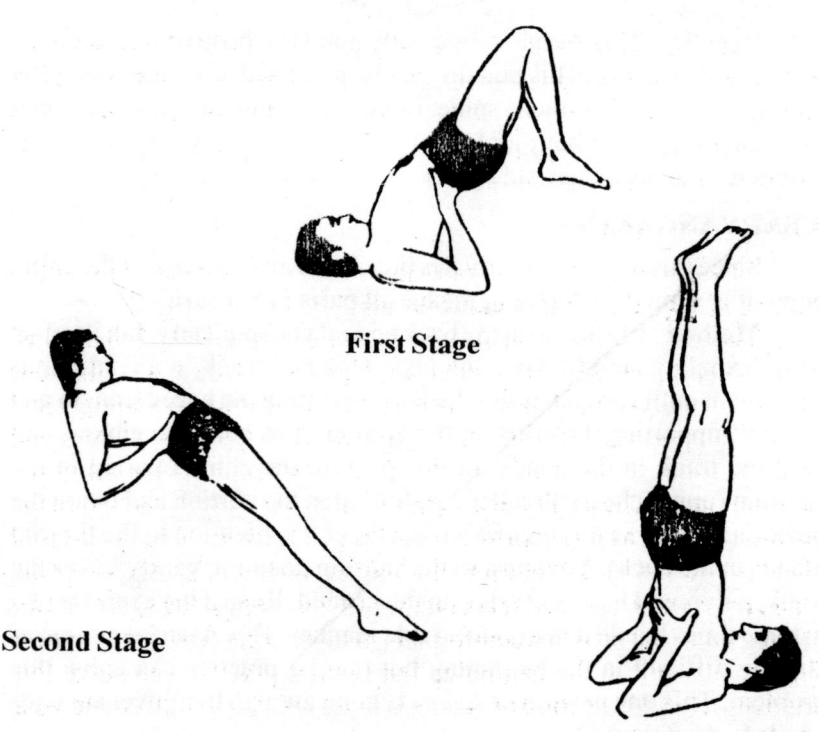

First Stage

Second Stage

Thrid Stage

Bhujangasana

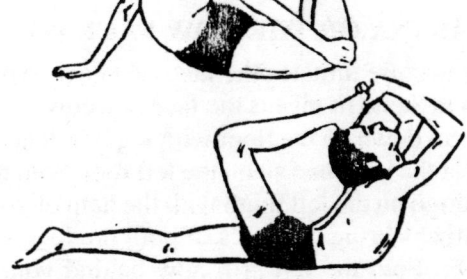

Benefits : This is a very rejuvenating exercise and cures whatever trouble is there in the back and shoulder region. This one asana does, by regular practice, wonder to the body. They say that the deposit of nectar is in the navel of man. But owing to the gravity-pull it goes down and get burnt in the gastric fire. But in this posture, whole of the nectar permeates every part of the body. Those who regularly practise this asana remain young and virile till ripe old age.

7. CHAKRASANA

In this asana the body takes the shape of a Chakra, hence the name.

Method : Lie flat on your back on a hard surface. Then, firmly fixing both the hands and feet on the ground raise the middle portion of the body upwards, making it form almost a semi-circle with the floor. Keep your head between your hands. While doing so, concentrate your eyes on any object lying in front of them.

Benefits : This asana, like the Sarvangasana, strengthens all the parts of the body, head, neck, throat, abdomen, hands, legs, etc. It eliminates pain in the joints, extra fat from the abdominal region and activates the digestive system. Its regular performance imparts glow and smartness to the body, prevents night discharge and makes the vertebral column supple and elastic. By performing this asana, the normal posture and stance of the body remains erect even in old age. It is not advisable for ladies to do it during pregnancy.

Note : (i) For the benefit of our readers, we are giving only those asanas or postures which can be performed even by a novice, without incurring any risk. That is why we are not including the king of the asanas, the Sheershasana' because its performance by a novice can incur more harm than good to the young performer's body. If one wants to do it or other difficult asanas, one is advised to consult other bigger books by our publishing house. (ii) The asanas given below are especially good for the females for preserving their vital statistics.

8. GOMUKHASANA OR THE COW FACE POSTURE

Since this posture imitates the face of a cow, it is known by this name. Gomukh in Sanskrit means the face of a cow.

Method : Sit down on the floor with legs stretched forward. Now fold the left leg at the knee and sit on the left foot. Fold the right leg and place the right thigh on the left thigh with the help of your hands. Now, lifting your buttocks bring the heels of both the feet together till they touch each other. Fold the left arm now behind your back over the shoulder. Fold the right arm behind the back but under the right shoulder.

Now bend the fingers of both the hand into two hooks to clasp each other. Remain in the pose with normal breathing for about 30 seconds. Keep your head and back erect and eyes glaring straight at some chosen point.

Gomukhasana

Repeat it reversing the position of legs and hands and maintain the pose again for 30 seconds. Then come out of the pose and relax. Do this exercise at least a couple of time with each hand. Whichever breast a lady wants to tone up, she must do this exercise with the hand of that side.

Benefits : This exercise strengthens the breast and shoulder muscles and makes the legs, muscle also more elastic. This exercise is good for males and females both.

9. KAGASANA OR THE CROW POSE

Kaga means a crow. Hence the name.

Method : Squat on the floor, keeping your arms between your legs and heels raised. Place the palms flat on the ground in front while keeping the arms in line and shoulders outstretched as much as you can. Now spread the fingers like claws, in front of you. Then raise your body on your toes and try to put pressure on your spread hands. Remain in the posture for 30 seconds to 1 minute, then come out of it. Do it on empty stomach, at least three to four times a day in one go.

Kagasana

Benefits : This asana not only helps to elongate your spine and diminish the unwanted arches on it, it strengthens your arms and shoulder muscles. This posture also helps in activating your harmonal discharges. Pregnant ladies or ladies of advanced age should not do this exercise.

10. KUKKUTASANA OR THE COCK POSE

A cock is called kukkut in Sanskrit, hence the name.

Method : Sit in Padmasana. Now insert your hands between the opening in your calves and thighs. Then push the hands further and keep your palms firmly planted on the floor with your fingers fully spread. Push your thighs and legs up your arms, using your arms as the fulcrum of exerting the force to lift your body up. Try to keep your torso as upright as possible. Breathe normally. Do it at least for a minute.

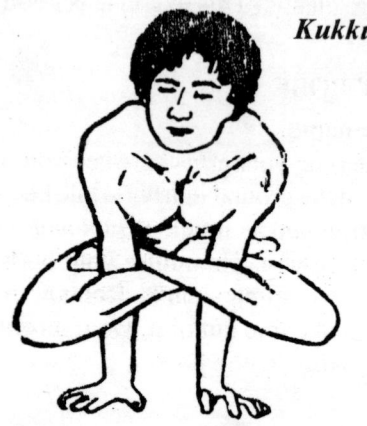

Kukkutasana

Benefits: As could be seen from the illustration, this posture puts enough pressure on your chest and shoulder muscles to make them firm. The females will have their firm breast line if they do this exercise regularly.

11. SHAVASANA OR THE CORPSE-POSE

Shava means a dead-body in Sanskrit. Hence this name. This asana is to be performed at the end of the exercise session as it helps body to get complete rest and bring peace to the mind.

Method : Lie down supine on a hard surface. Don't use any pillow. Let your body take the most naturally comfortable position. Now gradually begin to concentrate on each external limb of your body, starting from the toes. Try to convince yourself by auto-suggestion that your toes are quite relaxed. Try to move your toes a little and believe that they are so relaxed that you can't even move them. Gradually shift the focus of your mind to the upper limbs—feet, heels, shins, thighs, abdominal region, stomach, heart region, neck and finally, the head. Then relax and lie totally motionless like a dead-body. Close your eyes and try to be thoughtless. Remain in that position for about five minutes. By the time your end this exercise, your whole body and mind would have taken complete rest. Remain lying for a couple of minutes more and come gradually out of this trance-like state.

Benefits: As hinted already, this asana takes away the whole mental and physical stress and strain and revitalises your entire sense with an euphoria of a fully rested body.

D. AN INDEX OF THE YOGIC EXERCISE HELPING IN THE CURE OF CERTAIN DISEASES.

Disease	Yogasana
1. T. B. and asthma	Siddhasana, Sheershasana, Sarvangasana, Matsyasana, Ardha Matsyendrasana, Supta Vajrasana and Bhujangasana.
2. Diabetes	Sidhasana, Sheershasana, Sarvangasana, Matsyasana, Ardha Matsyendrasana, Halasan, Chakrasana and Mayoorasana.
3. Sex sublimation, pyorrhoea and colic	Siddhasana, Sheershasana, Sarvangasana, Matsyasana, Ardha Matsyendrasana, Padmasana, Vajrasana and pashchimottanasana.
4. Pain in the ears, eyes, and nose	Siddhasana, Sarvangasana, Matsyasana and Ardha Matsyendrasana.
5. Loss of menstruation, painful menstruation, Menorrhagia and the diseases related to the uterus and ovary	Sarvangasana, Shalabhasana, Pashchimottanasana and Bhujangasana. (These asanas should not be practised during pregnancy.)
6. Chronic bronchitis, cough, difficulty in breathing	Matsyasana and Shalabhasana.
7. Disorders of the digestive system	Sarvangasana, Vajrasana, Pashchimottanasana and Baddha Padmasana.
8. Enlargement of the liver and the spleen	Sarvangasana, Halasana, Mayoorasana and Baddha Padmasana.
9. Chronic Constipation	Halasana, Mayoorasana, Dhanurasana, Matsyasana and Padahastasana.
10. Hernia, Elephantiasis, shortness of a leg or of an arm	Garudasana, Trikonasana and Utkatasana.
11. Piles	Siddhasana, Pashchimottanasana, Sheershasana, Gomukhasana and Mahamudra.
12. Dysentery	Baddha Padmasana and Kukkutasan.
13. Rheumatism in the	Vrushchikasana, Sheershasana, Pashchim-

	Joints	ottanasana and Sarvangasana.
14.	Leucoderma	Sheershasana, Padmasana, Siddhasana, Simhasana, Gomukhasana, Vakrasana and Vrukshasana.
15.	Fatness (Obesity)	Mandukasana, Pashchimottanasana, Mayoorasana, Suptavajrasana, Dhanurasana and Ardha Matsyendrasana.
16.	High blood pressure	Vajrasana, Siddhasana, Padmasana, Matsyasana and Shavasana.
17.	Low blood pressure	Sarvangasana, Halasana, Vajrasana, Padmasana, Siddhasana and Pashchimottanasana.
18.	Throat-trouble	Matsyasana, Simhasana, Suptavajrasana and Sarvangasana.
19.	Headache	Pashchimottanasana, Halasana, Sarvangasana and Shavasana.
20.	Hernia	Matsyasana, Sarvangasana and Suptavajrasana.
21.	Heart-disease (Cardiac trouble)	Shavasana, Baddha Padmasana and Siddhasana.
22.	Insomnia	Sarvangasana, Shavasana and Surya Namakara
23.	Menstrual troubles	Dhanurasana, Matsyasana, Suptavajrasana and Pashchimottanasana.
24.	Drowsiness	Lolasana, Kukkutasana, Uttamangasana, Bakasana, Tolasana, Utthita Dwihastabhujasana and Utthita Ekapada Sheerasana.
25.	Intestinal diseases	Lolasana, Garbhasana, Baddhahasta Padmasan and Surya Namaskara.
26.	Lumar pain	Vakrasana, Tolangulasana, Halasana and Surya Namaskara.
27.	Dermatic diseases	Padmasana, Siddhasana, Simhasana, Veerasana, Utkatasana, Mandukasana, Suptavarjasana, and Vrukshasana.
28.	Diseases related to the chest and the lungs	Baddha Padmasana, Utkatasana, Sarvangasana, Viparitakarni, Sheershasana, Vrukshasana and Surya Namaskara.
29.	Fever, chronic fever	Garbhasana, Utthita Padmasana, Siddhasana, Gomukhasana and Shavasana.
30.	Impotence	Padmasana, Siddhasana, Simhasana, Ma-

	ndukasana, Vajrasana, Suptavajrasana and Gomukhasana.
31. Impurities of veins	Lolasana and Utthita Ekapada Sheerasana.
32. Leg-ailments	Baddha Padmasana, Utkatasana, Akarna Dhanurasana, Tolangulasana and Padmasana.
33. Kidney stone	Matsyendrasana, Matsyasana, Tolangulasana and Vajrasana.
34. Paralysis	Padmasana, Veerasana, Parvatasana, Matsyendrasana, Matsyasana, Siddhasana, Simhasana and Mandukasana.
35. Derangement of bile	Halasana, Vartulasana and Shalabhasana.
36. Morbid excitement, hysteria	Padmasana, Vakraasana, Ardha Matsyendrasana, Vrushasana, Mandukasana, and Vajrasana.
37. Leprosy	Padmasana, Matsyendrasana, Siddhasana, Simhasana, Gomukhasana and Veerasana.
38. Blood-impurities, Loss of blood	Lolasana, Kukkutasana, Bakasana, Utkatasana, Sarvangasana, Sheershasana and Vrukshasana.
39. Elephantiasis	Matsyendrasana, Utkatasana, Ekapada Sheerasana.

CHAPTER VIII

YOUR FOOD : GUIDELINES AND TABLES

The importance of diet in giving you good health can't be gainsaid. Food is the most basic requirement of any live body. But the Yogic-dictum is. "Just as over-eating makes the body fat and heavy, under-eating makes it weak and illness-prone. The proper balance must therefore be found between the needs of the body and the quantity of food eaten."

A well-balanced diet contains sufficient quality of protein, carbohydrates, fats, salts and minerals. It is held in Yoga discipline that "as you eat, so you become." This is because the kind and quality of food affects the physical as well as mental condition of the individual. In Yoga all foods have been divided into three categories : Rajasi (royal), Tamasi (baser or carnal) and Sattvik (noble). The rajasi food comprises a variety of dishes. This type of food includes fried, roasted and ghee-rish food, which is not desirable for good health. A little intake of these type should be sufficient to titillate the palate. A little quantity of strongly spiced bitter or sour food (tamasik) should also form part of diet which should mostly be made by easily digestible, nourishing and freshly prepared food which classifies the noble or Sattvik food. Your food must give you the variety of all the six varieties of taste, sweet, salty, astringent, bitter, sour and biting. However, it is not only the quantity or quality of the food but your way of eating it is also very important. Whatever food you eat, masticate it thoroughly and allow the saliva to reduce the eaten morsel to a mere pulp before gulping it down. Always eat 75 to 80% to your total capacity and leave enough room for the movement of gas/liquid etc. to help the system digest the eaten food quickly. Drinking water with food should be totally far gives. \drink water always half an hour before and half on hour after your having food. Drink lots of water between your meals but not 'with them.

For your help we give below some guidelines following which you shall remain healthy. Adherence to them will not only keep diseases and disorders at bay but enhance also the age of your healthy life.

(i) The food that we eat helps build the blood cells, nerves, bones and muscles in our body. It has been proved scientifically that food which is highly processed and high in protein, fat, salt and sugar leads to health problems. Nutritious food (balanced wholesome diet), moderate exercises, drinking enough—[8/10 glasses (3 litres)] water, enjoying fresh air and sunshine, resting adequately everyday will ensure a healthy body and healthy mind.

(ii) Overhaul/detoxify the system completely by fasting 2 to 4 days every three months with liquids, preferably fresh lemon water with honey 4-5 times daily and follow it up with an all-fruit course for 5 to 7 days and then resort to normal diet cautiously and gradually. Take enema on the days of fasting immediately after taking mud pack for 15/20 minutes. Also take abdominal pack at night.

(iii) Abdomen must be kept cool and soft always. All liquid intake should be close to the body temperature as far as possible. Take mud pack, hip bath, enema and oil massage intermittently.

(iv) Drink 1 or 2 glasses of water on rising, every morning.

(v) Dental health plays a vital role in causing a troubled addomen; an unhealthy abdomen is responsible for most of the diseases.

(vi) Use honey and molasses instead of sugar. Use a lot of garlic and some ginger if they suit. Take maximum roughage/fibre.

(vii) Avoid non-vegetarian concentrated, stimulating, intoxicating and gas forming food.

(viii) Ideal time for lunch is 10.00 a.m. and for dinner 7.00 p.m. May take some fruits (one variety only) around 2.00 p.m. Take only two meals a day and satisfy 80% of your hunger or appetite. Do not drink water during meal but take in plenty one hour after the meal. Chew well. Do not eat if not hungry or in bad mood/anger or at odd hours.

(ix) Shun-smoking, tea, coffee, alcohol, zarda, panmasala, soft drinks and drugs.

(x) Going for brish walk and/or doing. Yoga for 30 to 60 minutes daily—is a must.

(xi) Wash vegetables and fruits properly under running water, scrubbing with a brush before cutting, as they contain pesticides and contaminants. If any germs are suspected then wash in water with

diluted solution of potassium permanganate.
- (xii) Ensure good digestion, sound sleep, good appetite and evacuation of bladder and bowels regularly and naturally.
- (xiii) Tension is very harmful, as it causes flatulence, constipation, irritability, besides liver and heart problems. Hence, change the way of living. Do not work for long hours. Do not become a workaholic. Do Shavasan and enjoy minimum 7 hours sound sleep daily.
- (xiv) Always use polyunsaturated oil and reduce welt and sugar intake to the minimum possible level.
- (xv) After lunch, rest a while and after dinner, walk a mile—is a wise old recommendation. Relax in Vajrasan for 10-15 minutes after the meal.
- (xvi) Take very light but nutritious food which includes fruits, skimmed milk and yoghurt (curds).
- (xvii) For healthy condition, 80 per cent of alkaline foods to 20 per cent of acid foods are needed. For curative treatment, 100 per cent alkaline diet is needed. Alkaline food and drink purify the blood. Refined and processed food tend to acidify and pollute the blood and the cells.
- (xviii) Select your food from the following.
  - (a) **Acid producing foods :**
    All flesh foods, fish, pulses, white bread, polished rice, white flour, nuts, confectionery, sweets, coffee, tea, cocoa, alcohol, boiled buffalo milk, fried foods, concentrated foods, hydrogenated stuff, powder milk, chilled foods, cheese, white sugar, beans, onions, peanuts, tomatoes, jam and all preservatives, pickles, unripe fruits, refined stuff, grapes, high protein food.
  - (b) **Alkali producing foods :**
    All kinds of vegetables, potatoes, fresh fruits, butter-milk, fresh lemon, coconuts (tender), figs, dates, almonds, loquates, skimmed milk, yoghurt, molasses, olives, sweet oranges, dry fruits, sprouts, whole flour/unpolished rice, honey.
- (xix) It is suggested that one may keep the following items at home. They are negligible incost, but help in maintaining healthy body (of course, a support of exercises and balanced diet is prerequisite of Naturopathy) :

(a)	Hip bath tub	:	1 or 2 Nos.
(b)	Fomentation bags	:	2 or 3 Nos.
(c)	Abdomen/chest pack	:	1 set

(d) Mud tray and towel
(e) Enema Kit
(f) Bucket for hot foot bath
(g) Tumbler for *Jalneti*
(h) Infra-red lamp
(i) Facial steam kit

} 1 No. each

Thus we see that our senses and faculties sometimes work at cross-purposes, and throw the body out of gear. It can be brought back to normalcy by observing the simple do's and dont's enumerated above.

TABLE I - CALORIE CONTENT OF FOOD

1. CEREALS AND COOKED FOOD

	Quantity	*Calories*
Soup (normal)	1 cup	90
Cooked Rice	1 cup	130
Chapati (medium)	1	80
Poori	1	95
Prantha (plain)	1	145
Subji (vegetable curry) cooked in sunflower oil	1 cup	60
Idli	1	80
Dosa (plain)	1	125
Dosa (masala)	1	240
Vada and Sambar	1	140
Dal	1 cup	160
Papad (roasted)	1	40
Samosa (medium size)	1	140
Sweets (burfi of medium size)	1	100
Rasogulla (medium size)	1	120
Salted biscuits	4	100
Cream Crackers	3	100
Corn Flakes	1 cup	100
Sugar	1 tsp (5 gm)	20

	Quantity	Calories
Honey	1 tsp (5 gm)	16
Cereals and Pulses	100 gm	360
Toast with butter	1	100
Cooking oil like soya bean/ ground nut	3 tsp	135
Sunflower/Safflower oil	3 tsp	135

2. FRUITS AND VEGETABLES

	Quantity	Calories
Apple	100 gm	59
Banana	100 gm	116
Blue grapes	100 gm	58
Green grapes	100 gm	71
Mosambi	100 gm	43
Mango	100 gm	74
Watermelon	100 gm	16
Orange	100 gm	48
Papaya	100 gm	32
Pineapple	100 gm	46
Chikoo	100 gm	98
Seetafal	100 gm	104
Fruit juices (without sugar)	1 glass	125
Methi leaves	100 gm	49
Spinach (palak) leaves	100 gm	26
Beetroot, carrot	100 gm	45
Potato	100 gm	97
Gourds (ash, bitter, ridge, snake)	100 gm	10-25
Cabbage, Cauliflower	100 gm	30
Pumpkin	100 gm	25
Cucumber	100 gm	13
Ladies finger	100 gm	35
Green peas (fresh)	100 gm	93
Leafy vegetables	100 gm	32

	Quantity	Calories
Mixed salad	100 gm	70

3. MILK AND MILK PRODUCTS

	Quantity	Calories
Buffalo milk	1 cup	210
Cow milk	1 cup	130
Skimmed milk	1 cup	80
Milk shake	1 glass	210
Yoghurt (whole milk)	1 cup	100
Yoghurt (skimmed)	1 cup	60
Buttermilk	1 cup	30
Paneer	25 gm	100
Butter	1 tsp	35

4. MISCELLANEOUS

	Quantity	Calories
Almonds/Cashewnuts	10 pcs	100
Soft drinks	1 bottle	85
Tea/coffee with milk and sugar	1 cup	50
Ice Cream	1 cup	60

TABLE II
HEIGHT - WEIGHT TABLE
DESIRABLE WEIGHT - MEDIUM FRAME

ADULT MALE		ADULT FEMALE	
Height cm (ft.-in.)	Weight (kg)	Height cm (ft.-in.)	Weight (kg)
160 (5'-3")	59-62		
163 (5'-4")	59-63	50 (4'-11")	46-51
165 (5'-5")	60-64	152 (5'-0")	47-53
168 (5'-6")	61-66	155 (5'-1")	48-53
170 (5'-7")	63-68	157 (5'-2")	50-55
173 (5'-8")	65-70	160 (5'-3")	52-56
175 (5'-9")	66-71	163 (5'-4")	52-58
178 (5'-10")	67-73	165 (5'-5")	53-60
180 (5'-11")	70-75	168 (5'-6")	56-63
182 (6'-0")	71-76	170 (5'-7")	57-65

TABLE III
VITAMINS IN YOUR FOOD

Vitamin	Function in the body	Main source	Recommended daily allowances for adults
A (fat soluble)	Essential for normal growth and development, including bones and teeth. It protects body against disease especially that of the respiratory tract. Necessary for good sight, healthy skin and body tissue repair in general	Milk, curds, butter cheese, pumpkin carrots, leafy vegetables, tomato, mango, papaya orange, melon apricots, peaches potatoes.	5,000 I.U.
B1 or Thiamine (water soluble)	Plays important role in normal functioning of brain, heart nervous system. Regulator of carbohydrate metabolism. Regulates appetite and maintains good digestion.	Wheat germ, yeast outer layer of rice, wheat and other whole grain cereals especially after sprouting, nuts, peas, lime, soyabeans, dried, beans, legumes, soya, dark green leafy vegetables, milk, cheese, banana, apple, molasses.	1.2-20 mg
B6 or Pyridoxine (water soluble)	Helps in absorption of fats and proteins	Rice, milk, molasses, yeast, cereals, soya and fresh vegetables	2-3 mg

B12 (water soluble)	Essential for proper functioning of the central nervous system and proper utilisation of food for body building purposes	Soya Milk and cheese	3 mg
C Ascorbic Acid (water soluble)	Essential for normal growth and maintenance of practically all body tissues especially those having to do with joints, bones, teeth and gums. Protection against infections. Great help in quick healing of wounds	Citrus fruits like orange, lemon, tomato, grapefruit, mosambi, melon, potato and green leafy vegetables, cabbage, amla, sprouted bengal and green grams.	50-75 mg
D (fat soluble)	Essential for proper bone and teeth formation. Helps in the metabolism of calcium and phosphorus.	Rays of the sun, milk, butter, cheese	400-800 I.U.
E (fat soluble)	Essential for normal reproductory function, fertility and physical tone. Helpful in cardio-vascular diseases.	Wheat or cereal germ, whole grain products, green leafy vegetables especially lettuce alfalfa, milk, soyabeans	12 I.U.

TABLE IV
OILS AND FATS
It is the difference that counts

Type of oil or fat	Percent Polyun- saturated Fat	Percent Saturated Fat
Safflower (Kardi) Oil	74%	9%
Sunflower Oil	64%	10%
Corn Oil	58%	13%
Avergae Vegetable Oil (Soyabean+Cottonseed)	40%	13%
Sesame (Til Oil)	38%	13%
Chichen Fat*	26%	29%
Groundnut Oil	21%	19%
Average Vegetable Shortening	20%	32%
Mustard Oil	18%	6%
Lard*	12%	40%
Olive Oil	9%	14%
Beff Fat *	4%	48%
Butter*	4%	61%
Palm Oil*	2%	81%
Coconut Oil*	2%	86%
Ghee*	Nil	65%

All fats and oils are equally high in calories, so see how little you can be use. When you use fats and oils, choose those high in polyunsaturated fats—the ones at the top of the chart.

* Must be avoided.

TABLE V

The most important nutrients that the body needs, and some of the veg. foods which provide them

The body needs Nutrients for	These are called	They are found in
Building and repair of the body	Protein	Cheese, milk, buttermilk, curd, peas, beans, lentils, soya, nuts.

Building teeth and bones	Minerals (i) Calcium (ii) Phosphorus	Milk, cheese, flour, cabbage, baked beans, curry powder, dried fruits.
Transport of oxygen	Iron	Kelp, black molasses, cabbage, spinach
Vital for healthy nervous system and cell structure, helps promote, absorption and metabolism of protein and many vitamins.	Magnesium	Banana, leafy vegetables kelp, dolomite.
Energy	Carbohydrates (i) Starch (ii) Sugar (not needed for the body but often consumed)	Flour, rice, potatoes, cereals. Sugar, Jam, Syrup, sweets, chocolate, tinned foods.
	Fats	Butter, ghee, margarine, oil milk, cheese, chocolate.

CHPATER IX

TRADITIONAL NATUROPATHIC TREATMENT FOR VARIOUS DISEASES

Given in this chapter are the traditional treatments of the various disorders and disease for those readers who believe in the age-old maxim that "old is gold." Of course, should they want they can replace some of them with the treatments given in the preceding pages to find the ideal combination most suiting for their system. That is, may be, you find the wheat juice not as much suiting to your body-chemistry as the juice of the bottle-gourd etc. It is because this school of treatment treats every patient as an individual case. There are no patient remedy for the treatment of a particular disorder. What is given in these pages are the suggestion. You have to find your own 'locus' from the plethora of the variables available, i.e. your own body-chemistry vis-a-vis the intensity of the disorder etc. Since all these treatments are fool-proof—that is, having no side or adverse effects whatever—it is advisable to try all the remedies in order to hit upon the one most suiting to your body-chemistry. For example, there could be certain persons who might be allergic to garlic. In their case replacing garlic with any other base of the treatment—like ginger or lemon—would be eminently advisable. Of course if your have no such allergies you may go ahead with any kind of the treatment you like. Sometime some of you might not like the wet pact on your body owing to the particular allergy of your skin. So you must do the experiment to hit upon the remedy most compliable with your system.

1. DIGESTIVE DISORDERS

(a) **Indigestion or Dyspepsia**

   The basic causes of this disorder are weakness of the digestive system and over-eating. Over-eating results in lots of undigested food passing through the intestines and rectum, causing indigestion. Stools of such persons contain large amounts of undigested matter. They suffer from flatulence arising from putrefying matter in the stomach or in the intestine. Farting or belching may provide temporary relief, but there is generally a feeling of fullness amounting to heaviness, loss of appetite and general discomfort. Hyperacidity is also one of the symptom of such disorder which cause a burning sensation and even eructation.

Remedy : The chief remedy to this disorder is keeping the system light by fasting or taking a very frugal diet. Take bland food and lots of water to cure this malady. At times, heating your abdomen by means of hot-water bottle when your stomach is empty or after three hours of your having food. This fomentation can activate your digestive process. The procedure could be alternated with cold compresses, could help in accelerating the pace of recovery. Besides this palliative treatment, the patient can get long-lasting relief if he increase his body heat through various exercises. Avoid all the starchy food, rice, etc. Take plenty of water in-between the meals. Minimise the intake of alcohol and tobacco, and if you must have meat, scrape it down and keep it free from fat.

Normally indigestion is caused by having more food than your system can digest. The persons having easy-going life andsedantry habits often get afflicted with this disorder. Regular exercises and slight physical labour must form a part of your daily routine.

(b) **Constipation**

When the bowels are opened too seldom or incompletely such a malady results. Such persons pass hard stool, that too quite infrequently. They have desire to pass stool but unable to do so. The basic cause of this remedy is wrong way of life. Such persons eat heavy food and try to feel light by taking a variety of purgatives to relieve themselves. Some people have this feeling that unless they have adequate quantity of tea, they won't be able to defecate properly. If your body is unable to expel the waste matter, many foul gases emerge owing to putrification of undigested food. Retention of stools could lead to poisoning of the whole system. When the system fails to get rid of the waste matter, the persons take recourse to various purgatives and laxatives. Since these are all habit forming, you need more and more such drugs with increased potency, resulting in other ailments also.

Remedy : Light food, lots of water and salads and other easily digestible bland food are what you should take to cure such maladies. Your food must be made of two parts of fruits and vegetables and one part of the cereals. Top it by milk boiled only once. Eating more of low caloried food, like tomatoes, carrots, spinach and cabbage. If you are on the wrong side of forty, don't gave more than two meals a day. Eat light food and do regular exercise to get rid of this malady. You must walk at least 10 kms. a day if you can't do other rigorous physical exercise or run for about 3 kms. every day. At times people suffer constipation because their water intake is much less. Consume at least 250 mililitres of water a day. A glass of luke-warm water with drops of fresh lemon added to it is an ideal way of activating your bowels. Take mud packs or cool your abdomen by a towel soaked in cold water. Initially you might feel no urge to pass the stool. But make the habit of going to toilet twice a day whether you feel the urge to relieve yourself or not. Just in a day or two you'd start feeling it and that would be the symptom of your controlling the malady.

(c) **Dysentry**

Inflammation and ulceration of the lower portion of bowels results in this malady which is also called the bloody flux. Pain in the limbs, slight fever, colicky pain in the abdomen followed by diarrhoea are some of the symptom of this malady. At times the stools have traces of blood. Bacillary dysentry suddenly affects the system while amoebic dysentry comes gradually leading to loss of weight and anaemia. The aggravated malady also has the intestines perforated, accompanied by severe haemorrhage.

Remedy : Fasting with only lukewarm water taken during fasting is a sure cure of this malady. When the discharge of mucus with stools starts, warm water enema should be taken. Mud pack could also be a very effective treatment. Light, frugal food with very little or no cereals should be taken. Avoid all fried, roasted, ghee-smeared rich food. Avoid sugar also, take honey if you feel like taking some sweet thing. In certain chronic cases the curd-treatment might be needed but complete rest is advised throughout the treatment. Light exercise and walking might be taken up after a couple of days.

(d) **Ulcers and Acidity**

When hydrochloric acid present in the stomach increase in quantity, the condition is known as hyperacidity which, too, gives rise to gastritis and ulcer—gastric, peptic and duodenal. Dietetic indiscretion, indigestion of heavy meals, addiction to alcohol and amoking might be the chief cause to afflict body with this malady. Dizziness, nausea, eructation and loss of appetite are some of its amin symptoms. Serious complications, like haemorrhage, perforation and obstruction of the pylorus (the orifice through which food passed from stomach to the intestines) also appear. Worry, anger, tension, jealously and hurrying aggravate or sometimes start the trouble.

Remedy : Shun all the spicy, seasoned and fried, roasted with oil or ghee food plus alcoholic drinks. Milk, cream, butter, fruits and boiled vegetables are the best diet for such a patient. Have more of pithy fruits like bananas, mangoes, mush melons and dates. If the trouble is chronic, shun all the cereals and have just 300 ml. of milk with fruits. Just a banana and once-boiled milk should be taken as the first food in the morning. Avoid leafy vegetables and vegetables with their rind on as they might create friction in the stomach. Take Isabgol with water or milk after every meal. Hip bath for 10 to 15 mts. will also help tremendously. Whether you take hip bath or place mud-pack, do so on empty stomach. Have your daily massage and do deep breathing exercises.

(e) Flatulence

Excessive wind formation in the stomach, rumbling sound assuring from the insides after meals are some of the main symptoms of the malady. Persons who don't masticate their food and gulp down the unchewed food often suffer from this disorder. One should shun eating sweets, sour and refined foodstuffs or else the trouble will continue. Take only fruits for breakfast and boiled vegetables for lunch for some days. Emphasis should be on light, easily digestible food, preferably uncooked as much as possible.

Remedy : Musticating your food properly is an ideal remedy to cure this disorder. Saliva must be properly mixed with food before you gulp it down. The another advantage of musticating your food properly is that you just can't eat more. Your jaws would be somewhat tired. That is why it is held in ancient Indian belief "that 'drink' your food while 'eat' your water!" It means you must chew your food as much as to make it almost liquid - like and drink water slowly and gradually. Gulping food and drinking water in one go take along some unwanted air with your food and drink, which creates trouble when trapped inside. Have light food, masticate it properly and eat at regular interval for the early recovery from this trouble.

(f) Piles

When the veins about the lower end of the bowels develop inflamed conditions, one is known to be suffering from piles or haemorrhoids, which sometimes appear externally, internally or in the mixed form. In external haemorrhoids there is no bleeding but much pain, while in the internal ones there is discharge of dark blood with less pain. Piles, actually is rather a symptom than a disease. The disease is chronic constipation which results in the appearance of haemorrhoids. The pressure applied in voiding constipated bowel tends to distend the views and a external piles may be swollen causing pain. A person afflicted with piles may not be able to sit properly.

Remedy : Since the basic cause of piles is constipation efforts should be made to cure the basic ailment rather than treat the symptoms. Care should be taken the your stool doesn't get hardened. The best diet to secure a soft stool will comprise wheat porridge, whole wheat—bread, green vegetables—gourds of various kinds, spinach, radish, carrots, etc., fruits like papaya, ripe banana, musk melon, pears—topped by milk. Soak the big sultanas ('Munakka') in water overnight and eat it on empty stomach, drink the water sultanas were soaked in with few drops of fresh lemon mixed into it. You can supplement your diet with dry fruits— about 200 gms. at a time.

(g) **Diabetes**

Diabetes or Diabetes Mellitus is normally caused by harmonal disturbance. When the pancreases become inactive or atrophied to produce the desired quantity of insulin to convert sugar in the food into energy, the patient suffers this disease. This disease is basically of a disorder of assimilation of food. Despite having voracious appetite and eating rich food, the patient continues to grow weak and emaciated. The weakened system has its resistance and the vital force ebbing drastically, causing the appearance of boils or carbuncles on the skin which take long time to heal. Eczema and itching of groin together with, in the aggravated state, gangrene of the toes are some of the symptoms. The patient might feel unusually thirsty during the night.

Remedy : Naturopathy treats the disease not by drugs but with proper control of diet. Assimilation of sugar by the body should be the main aim to achieve. The ideal diet for such a patient would be 1 kg. of curd made from cow's milk and various kinds of gourds, bitter or sweet with little of salt, followed by juices of citrus fruits and consumption of oranges, pineapple, rose apple (*Jamun*). The person afflicted with this disease must take long walks to activate his pancreas. Hip bath, light physical exercise and long walks on foot help in speedy recovery of such patients. Sweets, fried food are bad for such persons. Germinated black grams, about 50 gms. daily help the system regain its power of assimilation.

(h) **Worms**

The little parasites that infest human intestines are known as worms. They are of four types: threadworm, tapeworm, hookworm and roundworm. Persons having these worms have voracious appetite but despite their devouring large quantity of food they appear weak and emaciated. They don't gain weight. Out of these four, threadworm is the most common malady, which normally afflict children more. They breed in the intestine because of the dirty habits of the afflicted persons who don't wash their hands properly before taking their food; don't wash their hands after touching any dirty, filthy objects. Sometimes using the garments of the afflicted person also transmit this problem. Often children afflicted with this problem long for eating sweets. Since they get itching in their anus after defecating, they scratch it quite often.

Remedy : The allopathic drugs the traditional treatment might provide temporary relief, but there is no permanent remedy for this ailment in their system of the medicines. Treat such a patient with teaching him how to live cleanly. The child suffering it must be given warm enema to which a half-lime's juice is added, followed by administration of about 50 to 100 ml. of coconut oil with the help of a syringe through the anus. Ask the child to exert a little pressure on the system while defecating. The ideal treatment should be complete fasting with lukewrarm enema in the morning and evening. Then give the child a diet consisting of fruits and boiled vegetables for five six days. Tomatoes roasted over coal should be administered on the empty stomach. Milk and cereal-diet should be prohibited for such a patient. Raisins soaked in water may by slao given as the last edible thing before the patient goes to sleep. Mud packs applied between the navel and pubes also help. Juice of garlic is an ideal remedy for such a trouble.

2. FEVERS

When the body temperature shoots up higher because of some internal disturbance in the system, the person is said to be suffering from fever. Fevers are basically of two types : seasonal fever, that which afflicts one owing to change of season or some minor, temporary disturbance, and others are symptomatic—that which one has owing to one's catching some germs or some infection or due to some major disturbance in the body-system. If the temperature of the body reaches

105° F tne term is hyperpyrexia (high fever). The onset of fever may be mild or severe depending upon the disease which has caused it or whose cardinal symptom it is. Generally, the fever is a warning symptom which tells there is something wrong in the body. Hence fever is believed more to be 'friend' than a 'foe.' Normally, ordinary fever has its fixed course and it should not be suppressed as the suppression might result in one's having some major ailment. Fever is a natural crisis and it must be helped to run its normal course ; any interference, such as administration of drugs, is only likely to retain the poison which caused the crisis. The onset of feve kills the patient's appetite, it is a natural phenomenon, hence fasting is the most likely first step.

Nothing should be eaten during the fever, or just a very light variety of food, that too if the patient wants it. If the body has to divert a part of those energies towards the digestion of food which in most cases is forced on the patient because the physician thinks that his strength is to be maintained, the only result it that the course of nature is obstructed and more complications are created.

Now we'll take up only those kinds of fever which results out of some external agency causing internal disturbance in the body.

(i) **Influenza**

Cardinal Symptoms : High temperature, aches over the whole of the body, stiffness of the limbs and a sore throat. The fever originates through a lowering of the vitality of the individual. Like all other diseases, it is a natural attempt of the body to clean itself. Only the wrong type of medicines complicate the matters. If broncho-pneumonia develops after during the last stage of influenza the poison may spread to the heart and can even cause cuganosis leading to death.

Remedy : Treat the fever caused by influenza—affliction like you treat all the fevers. The minor difference being: fasting should be undertaken for five to seven days depending upon the elevation of temperature of the body. After the fast the patient should be kept on all-fruit diet for a couple of days. Milk and fruits may be allowed thereafter followed by boiled vegetables.

(ii) **Malaria**

It is a typically tropical fever, caused by a germ which enters the blood stream through the bite of a mosquito of a particular variety. Just before the onset of malaria the patient has vague pains all over the body, headache and a slight rise of temperature. The onset of fever is preceded by a feeling of chilliness in the hottest weather and no amount of blankets or quilts give any relief from the chill. After several hours of high temperature, the sweating begins and the fever comes down leaving the patient extremely weak and emaciated. The fever might relapse after a day or two days or more.

Remedy : The treatment of malaria is the same as for all the fevers. If temperature shoots up beyond 105°F, wrap the patient in a sheet dipped in iced water to bring down the fever, till fever is 102°F or nearabout. No milk should be given to the patient. Loss of appetite is a natural consequence of malaria; it is a nature's way of warning the system "not to take any so-called nourishment"! Give the patient water, as much as possible or in the cases where the patient feels acute weakness, orange juice may also be given. Fasting is the natural desire of the patient and it should be maintained. When fever begin to drop, it means the poison in the body is lessening. But the patient should continue to fast till the danger of reappearance of the fever is past.

(iii) **Typhoid Fever**

It is a typical fever having a fixed course of temperature, marked by abdominal symptoms consisting of ulceration of the bowels, an eruption on the skin, an uncertain duration and chances of frequent relapses. It starts very mildly, then gradually develops with marked symptoms of headache, lassitude and insomnia, feverishness particularly at night. The temperature rises in the evening and falls in the morning. Each succeeding day the highest and the lowest point tends to increase till the disease has run its course. Ulceration of the bowels may lead to haemorrhage. In naturopathic cure, typhoid fever is hit in the limbs having accumulated waste and the petrefying material. The target is the toxic material causing it.

Remedy: The patient should be asked to take fast till the temperature comes down to normal. Only water and orange juice may be administered during the course of the fever. When the fever vanishes, put the patient on all fruit diet and take dietary precaution to prevent its relapse. Then, after a couple of days, give the patient boiled vegetables and unrefined foods like the whole wheat bread and unmilled rice. Even after the fever is fully cures, the patient should take full precaution and avoid rich food, etc.

3. RESPIRATORY DISORDERS

(i) **Common Cold**

It is also known as coryza or catarrh of the nose. Although its occurrence is quite common, yet it is quite irritating. It results out of sudden change of the temperature your body is coming in contact with.

In hot season, people are wont to take cold-bath or drink cold water, not caring for the heat they feel and the profuse sweeting they experience. Any such drastic changes of the temperature effect your body adversely. In no other branch of medicine there's any cure for it. The doctors practising the allopathic system of medicine do say. " Common cold is cured in just a week's time if you take our medicine, otherwise it might take seven long days !"

Remedy : Naturopathy maintains that a cold is the result of inappropriate diet. It is nature's way of expecting poisonous humours from the body. The effect of the cold might last just for two to three days during which a patient must keep fast. Take half a kg. of spinach, 250 gms. of turnip, 250 gms. of tomatoes, 75 gms. of coriander leaves and 25 gms of ginger. Cut them to small pieces and boil them in a litre of water. When the vegetables turn tender, press them in muslin cloth and bring out their juices. Add a little salt, fresh lemon-juice and take it regularly with two hourly intervals in a tumbler to get this malady cured.

(ii) **Whooping Cough**

All food which produce phlegm is a taboo in this ailment. The patient should not be given milk, ghee, sweets, rice, refined flour products, sugar and lentils. The main diet should have oranges, musk-melon, tomatoes and raspberry. Boiled spinach, cabbage and gourds should be taken without mixing any condiments. Roasted potatoes, "wholewheat bread can be given. Fasting for two days and then administration of this diet to the patient can cure him in just three four days, time." Normally children get afflicted with this disease and they should be kept aloof as it is a contagious disorder.

(iii) **Tonsilitis**

Two almond shaped glands situated at either side of the narrow passage where the mouth joins the throat are known as tonsils. Although until recently they were believed to be useless, their importance against guarding infection is now an established fact. The inflammation of these glands is known as tonsilitis, which develops all of a sudden with accompanying pain in swallowing and sensation of chilliness. The fever shoots rather high and either one or both the tonsils become enlarged, emitting a grey material, which is a purulent discharge from the tonsils themselves. Tonsilitis is generally proceeded by coryza.

Remedy : The best way to deal with this ailment is to stop taking all solid food—only orange juice, lime juice and honey and water should be given to the patient. An enema should be taken daily so that all the waste matter is expelled from the body. No food which gives acidic effect should be given. A bath in lukewarm water or better still having cold and hot baths alternatively helps. Saline hot water gargles brings immediate relief. Chest and throat packs should also be resorted to. Massaging the neck and the backbone can help reduce the virulence of the attack. The patient should be kept on all-fruit diet even after the cure for a few days.

(iv) **Asthma**

Asthma is caused by excess of phlegm and inability of the body to expel it. The patient should immediately give up the food which enhances the phlegm-production in the body like milled rice, refined wheat, lentils, milk and curds, etc. Asthma is a disorder of the respiratory system characterised by severe paroxysm of difficult breathing.

Treatment : The patient should be given that type of food which helps contain the phlegm in the body. Feet him orange, tomatoes, papaya, guava, mango, jamun and carrots in the breakfast with dinner and lunch confined to only boiled vegetables. If the patient is not hungry dont' force any food down his throat. He may take a cup of warm water after every two hours, followed by hot enema. An asthma patient should regularly fast once a week and take an enema the morning after the fast to clear his bowels. Soaking of feet with warm water will provide immediate relief.

(v) **Bronchitis**

Inflammation of the bronchial tube that which joins the throat with the lungs is known as bronchitis. This inflammation also tends to impede the process of beathing owing to the sticking of phlegm inside the tube.

Remedy : Fasting is the only alternative in this ailment. Although the treatment outlined for asthma could also be useful in this disorder, there is slight change in the order of the items prescribed. Give the patient water and orange juice. When the fever is normal, the patient can also take all food diet. A hot Epsom salt bath every night or alternative nights will be beneficial during the acute stage of the disease. Towels soaked in hot water and applied to the chest are also helpful to release the sticking phlegm from the tube. Spinal manipulation under the guidance of a trained naturopath should be taken recourse to in chronic cases.

4. SKIN TROUBLES

(i) **Eczema**

Eczema is one of the most common diseases of the skin in India. It is manifest in the inflammation of the skin. Papules, vesicles and pustules get formed over the skin with more or less discharge. As a matter of fact eczema denotes the reaction of the skin to various forms of irritation. The root cause of this trouble, besides being the external erruptions, lies in the defective excretion of the bowels or kidneys. Eczema is of three types: dry, weeping or rubrum where it affects only the leg.

Remedy : The chief remedy of this skin disorder lies in cleansing the blood and the body of the afflicted. The patient must live in a well ventilated room. He or she should give up wearing tight-fitting clothes. The patient must consume three litres of water and must take bath twice a day. Rub your skin vigorously with your palm before taking bath. Clean all parts of your body thoroughly with water and then rub your palm against your body to dry the skin. Towel should not be used to dry your body. Alternate your bath with the sun-bath. Do it at least twice a week and then apply coconut oil over your skin afflicted with eczema. But never rub the parts having the actual site of eczema.

(ii) **Acne**

The skin disorder afflicting the sebaceous gland is known as acne. It occurs in both men and women, in their face at their puberty age, i.e. between 13 yrs. and 18 yrs. The condition is often accompanied by constipation and lack of fresh air aggravates the trouble. The eruption itself consist of little black spots which indicate the mouth of small sebaceous ducts chocked with dust or dirt.

Remedy : The ideal remedy for this ailment is dietary restrictions. The afflicted person should have only fruits and vegetables in his diet. Take plenty of exercise and ample quantity of water so that the morbid matter is ejected out through the bladder. Take raw cucumber, tomatoes, carrots, spinach and cabbage. A few months regulated diet would cure you of this trouble. External treatment by taking steam on your face also helps. Have the steam from boiling water on your face to open the pores of your facial skin. Dip a swab of cotton in fresh juice of lime and rub it on your face gently. Let the juice dry on your face. Then wash it clean after 10 mts. It will not only remove the dirt but open the pores also fully. Lemon juice is a very effective skin-freshner.

(iii) **Falling of the Hair**

It is also a common trouble. If the hair loss is due to any particular ailment. It shall duly stop the moment you are cured of the disease. In case it is caused when your body is healthy then you must try the following remedy.

Remedy : Some people have unusually oily skin. If that be the case then stop using oil altogether. Rub your hair with half a lemon and apply its juice liberally over your hair at least 15 mts. before your taking bath. Never wash your head with very hot water. In case you have dry skin, then a massage of the 'Anwla' oil once a week will help your hair grow long and sturdy.

(iv) **Baldness**

This malady is the advanced form of the malady discussed above. If it is due to skin trouble or is alopecia areata, it might effect the hair all over your body. However, the normal baldness is caused by the disturbance caused in the veins carrying blood to the skin.

Remedy : If you have oily skin, shun using oil completely. The best way to take care of your hair is to wet them thoroughly and allow them to dry. When they are partially dry, comb them first lightly then vigorously. Massaging your scalp with lemon juice 15 mts. before bath must become your daily ritual.

5. HEART AILMENTS

The chief ailments of heart are the following :

(a) Inflammation of the muscle, the outer and inner covering of the heart.
(b) Hardening of the arteries and formation of clot (thronbosis).
(c) Weakening of the muscle or degeneration of the organ because of advancing years.
(d) Heart ailment caused by rheumatism or suppression of syphilis.
(e) Pain in the chest behind the sternum, also known as angina pectoris.

In case you are non-vegetarian, then you should have only steamed fish or boiled white meat. Avoid fatty meat, especially pork. At times an overful stomach puts pressure on the diaphragm by flatulence and the pain of angina might start. The heart patient must realise that overloading your belly with rich food can aggravate the trouble, while fasting provides much wanted relief. They should fast for a short period according to their physical strength and never overtax your system. A heart patient should eat so sparingly that he should feel hungry all the time. Always have your last meal at least three hours before you go to sleep.

Another precaution that a heart patient should take is to prevent constipation as much as he can. He must take recourse to enema to get rid of constipation. A little exercise of a very light variety or walking for about a kilometer or so every day is a must for such a patient. Gravity douche or hot enema can be taken. Many doctors now realise the advantage of walking. When one walks the pressure on the heart is considerably reduced, because the blood going back for purification through the heart to the lung flows back easily when you are walking. It is not so when your are sitting or lying down. Besides walking you must have Epsom salt bath once or twice daily.

A heart patient must avoid all stress on his heart. Although all the doctors casually say that a heart patient must shun 'hurry, worry and curry,' it is not possible to avoid worry in a modern complex life. But one should try to reduce it as much as possible. And the heart patient if he or she wants to resort to naturopathic therapy, he or she must avoid taking all the drugs and other harmful medicines. Normally the human heart is capable of taking 400 times more load than it is designed to take. We might not realise the amount of work done by the heart nonstop for the entire life. Hence efforts should be made to stress it as little as possible.

When an attack is on, the best thing is to apply hot towels over the heart region. This will provide instant relief by reducing the constriction around the afflicted person's heart, by dilating (through heart) the clogged artery which finds it difficult to pass the required amount of blood through it to the heart.

Remedy : The ideal way to deal with all the heart diseases is to start a diet that cleanse your blood. All the impiety running in the blood is the chief cause of the heart ailments. Because, the cleaner the blood, the less will be the chance of any toxicity building up around the region of heart. The patient should take only fruits and vegetables. He should take two orange, an apple, grated carrots and beet-root together with some boiled vegetables and wholewheat bread. Avoid all the fats, ghee, butter, etc. and if you can't live without some butter, have it a little of it, preferably fresh and not the tinned one. Similarly eat no salt or very little of it.

6. TROUBLES CONNECTED WITH BLOOD CIRCULATION
(i) High Blood Pressure

In the modern life replete with all sort of troubles and tensions, the most damaging disease is High Blood Pressure or hypertension, Damaging, because without any apparent sign of illness, it reduces the patient to just being a bundle of nerves. Its causes include kidney disease, disorders of the endocrine glands and malfunctioning or disorders of the arteries. A congenital abnormality of the aorta is one of the most serious forms of hypertension. Its main symptoms are headaches, usually in the back of the head, ringing in the ears and giddiness. High Blood Pressure could be termed as mother disease because it gives rise to a plethora of ailments. The normal blood pressure should be 100 mm + age (systolic) and 80 mm plus age (diastolic).

Remedy : High B.P., according to naturopathy is the result of the accumulation of poisonous matter in the system. The remedy for it is: living on fruits and vegetables for at least a week. The best course would be to take fruit diet at five hourly intervals, i.e., only thrice a day. Have oranges for break fast, guava for lunch and tomatoes and apples for dinner. Besides, have pineapples, jamuns, musk melons, mangoes if you still feel hungry. After a week of 'fruits only' diet, milk should be added to it. Rub your body for five-seven minutes after you have taken your bath. Have bath in the water not very cold, but it should be of your body temperature. Keep your bowels clean and sleep well.

(ii) **Anaemia**

It is a condition where the amount of blood in the body is less than normal. Its symptoms are paleness of skin, a wan face, disinclination towards work of any kind, loss of appetite and general lack of well-being. It is caused by many factors: loss of blood due to injury, menstruation in excessive quantities, haemorrhage from piles, defective blood formation due to infection, toxins, and drugs, inadequate intake and lack of iron in the body.

Remedy : As is apparent from its causes, what a patient lacks in his body is fresh red blood. Hence your diet is to replenish the deficiency. For this the patient must have vegetable greens which are rich in Chlorophyll, such as spinach, bran of wheat, raisins, carrots, oranges and dates. Besides taking these fruits and vegetables, the sufferer must do adequate exercise. Sun-bathing in the morning for about a quarter of an hour daily is also a way to store up the elements that fight anaemia. The patient must bathe in cold water in the morning and rub his body dry with the palms of his hands. The anaemia patient must have his full quota of sleep and remain cheerful. If anaemia is symptomatic manifestation of some disease, then first try to cure those ailments—like chronic malaria, bleeding piles, syphilis or loss of blood due to injury.

(iii) **Jaundice**

When the bile-pigment lies in deeper layers due to deposition of a yellow pigment, the malady is known as jaundice. It is usually the result of malfunctioning of the liver, one of the five vital organs of the body. The other vital organs are the brain, the heart, the lungs and kidneys. The onset of jaundice may begin by loss of sleep, appetite, uneasiness and indigestion. The patient may feel chilly and have a constant feeling of nausea. Since liver in jaundice loses its capacity to dissolve the fat into nutrient for the body such a condition results.

Remedy : The prime aim of treating a jaundice patient is to see that his liver is not at all burdened. The best course is fasting and this will mean not starving the patient. The theory is : if you stop indigestion of food, the excretion of waste and morbid matter can be encouraged by freeing the system of the burden of digesting it. Juices of fruits and vegetables and water should be taken during fasting. Warm water enema must also be taken to rid the bowels of all the waste matter. When you see the improvement in the patient—the colour of the skin and the eyes would quite evidently prove it—fresh fruits juice or fresh juice could also be taken. When the virulence has abated, wholewheat or gram bread, boiled vegetable and salads can be taken. Juice of lime mixed with raisins, figs and fresh ripe fruit should be taken.

(iv) **Gout**

When the excess of uric acid in the blood manifesting itself by inflammation of joints with deposition of urate of soda, the malady is termed as gout which is a form of rheumatism. Naturopathy believes that like all other diseases, gout is the result of inadequate excretion of the morbid and poisonous matter from the orifice of the body.

Remedy : For the treatment of gout, it must be ensured that all the outlets of the body are functioning normally. The patient should breathe fresh air so that oxygen is available to him in larger quantities, cleansing his blood of poisonous humours. The gout patient must drink a lot of water to produce more urine and thus expel the toxic material from the body. He should take lukewarm water in the morning and evening mixed with the juice of lime. The pores of the skin should be activated by cold bath day and drying of the body with vigorous rubbing with the palms of the hand. Sun-bathing should be undertaken to produce sweat.

The patient should cover his head with a wet towel to save it from the excessive heat of the sun. Spending half an hour in the sun will activate the sweat glands. A cold-bath is very refreshing after a sun-bath. In case the patient is not willing to have cold-bath, he may wipe his sweat with a wet towel. The food for such a patient must have fresh fruits and wholewheat bread, i.e. those things which do not stick to the intestines.

7. NERVOUS DISORDERS

Nervous disorders are rather difficult to diagnose because the whole system remains hidden from the eye of the physician. He can know it only from the disturbances of the organs governed by the afflicted nerves. Under this category comes many maladies like apoplexy, forgetfulness, hysteria, mental defectiveness, mental illness, neuresthenia and others.

The most common disorder under this head are nervous weakness, nervous breakdowns or nervous exhaustion.

There could be many causes for nervous disorders, such as the loss of a dear one, money reverses, accidents and the like. The organic diseases may be apparent from an autopsy but the inorganic disorders manifest themselves in the shape of hysteria, anxiety states and nervous breakdowns. The nervous weakness can give rise to diseases like dyspepsia or palpitation which can't be helped by remedies directed towards those organs. These might effect a sudden change in the bodily functions like sudden loosening of bowels or bladder in case of fright. The persons suffering from these maladies generally experiences a nameless fear, agitation, perplexity, confusion, worry, disappointment, loneliness, irritability and insomnia. The physical symptoms are constipation, dyspepsia, headaches, vagueaches and pains all over the body and feverishness. The patient becomes hypochondriac. The typical fear is that if the patient hears about any disease he feels he is afflicted with it.

Remedy : Rest and sleep are the ideal for the person afflicted with these disorders. Sleep in day also for some hours. Try to relax and let your nerves derive strength. Actually the root cause of such disorders lies in the mind. Since a healthy mind can reside only in a healthy body, see that the body regains its health. The loosening of tensions by relaxation will help his organs to do their work properly and he would be able to get rid of the poisons. The patient, besides sleeping and taking adequate rest, must also do light exercises. Human body is a physical existence and to make it fall asleep, it must be a little tired. You sleep well when you are somewhat tired and exhausted. The patient should take walks and if possible, take to jogging. He must have light food which should include bread made from wheat from which bran has not been sieved out, fruits and boiled vegetables. Since nervous debility shows a marked lack of vitamin B, it should be eked out by its inclusion in his diet. Unpolished rice, milk, cucumbers, mangoes, pears, pineapples, guava, tomatoes, raisins and leafy vegetable should be his mainstay. He should be asked to eat his food in a relaxed manner, chewing it properly before swallowing it down.

Massages help a lot in such disorders. These massages help reduce the tension one's body is suffering from. Hydropathic treatment is also very effective. During his bath, the patient's back should be washed with a powerful shower-jet for a couple of minutes daily. Do so twice in summers and once in winters.

The patient must be psychological treated to make him regain his confidence. Restoration of his confidence would mean his getting cured of this nervous debility. Besides this treatment, he should do following yogic exercises which help in keeping his swkin firm yet supple.

Stand at ease with your both feet are just a feet apart. Now lock your hands and extend your arms downwards, upwards and backwards. Move the arms with the hands joined in a circular motion while inhaling and exhaling deeply during the movement. It would be better if the patient does these exercises under the supervision of a naturopath who must also be an Yoga expert.

In such disorders, the first causality is sleep invariably. With the result, due to lack of sleep or insomniac condition the patient feels run down and weak. A warm both before the patient's retiring to sleep is very effective. The patient must remember the following measures which are very effective to induce sleep.

You must have his bed room clean, airy and his clothes loose fitting. Try to read a light-story book or any book of your choice before you retire. The cardinal principle of having good sleep is: that mentally, you must cut yourself off from your present. Remember some happy event of the past and try to recreate the whole circumstances mentally from ab initio. It could be some pleasant journey, some happy event of your past—anything that can draw your mind away from the present.

At times the patient is unable to sleep because he feels mentally very charged up. If such a situation, he must wash his feet with slightly warm water and cover his head with a towel soaked in cold water.

Besides taking these physical cares, try to instil confidence in the patient. He must have will to recover, only then he can be fully cured.

8. SEXUAL DISORDERS

(i) Menstruation Problems

Normally girls and ladies have menstruation which last for three to five days and begins around 12-13 years of the female's age to end at 45 to 50 years. In the majority of healthy women the normal menstrual cycle is of twenty-six to thirty days with the exception connected with childbirth. Mainly the problems connected with menstruation are three types: amenorrhoea (the absence of menstruation); menorrhagia (excessive bleeding during menses); dysmenorrhoea (bleeding with pain during the menses).

Remedy : The prime aim to fight this remedy is to check the aberration in bleeding. According to naturopathy, this malady is also the result of some toxic material lying in the body. Such a patient would do well if she takes regulated food and balanced diet. The breakfast of the patient should include milk and fruit and her lunch and dinner should comprise of wholewheat bread, boiled vegetables with a lot of roughage and at least two to three litres of water in a day. Condiments and seasonings should be totally given up since they tend to produce acidity and increase costiveness. Walking and light exercise should be taken regularly. It would be better if a hip bath is taken before one goes for a walk or takes exercises.

(ii) **Leucorrhoea**

When a watery discharge from the uterus has white clot like substance having thick appearance, the malady is known as leucorrhea or the whites. It is caused by some infection occurring after child-bearing or even otherwise.

Remedy : The first and foremost requirement to fight this disease is to make the patient take up exercises which involve running or playing games like badminton or tennis. Spice and condiments should be avoided as they tend to produce irritation in the membranes. Adequate sleep, physical exercise, taking bath in cold water and drying your body with your palm are some of the measure that a lady must take to fight this disorder. They should shun eating polished rice and fish as they tend to increase the mucus content of the humours of the body. Whole-meal flour and greens should form the major part of your diet. Vegetables like carrots, tomatoes, onions, radishes, etc. should be eaten raw. Take sun-bath every day for two times.

(iii) **Nocturnal Emission**

It is one of the most common feature with the growing boys and as such can't be taken as a disease or disorder. But the old quacks have instilled such a fear that even the learned boys frequent clinic of the doctors. At the outset it must be clearly understood that it is not an abnormal symptom. Involuntarily discharge of semen during sleep or nocturnal emission is not a disease. However its frequent recurrence does reflect upon the mental and physical health of the boy. If that be the case, i.e. if it occurs three to four times a week then the following treatment is recommended.

Remedy : Get up early in the morning. Visit the toilet, take a bath and go for a long walk. Then take a sun bath at about 7 a.m. The breakfast should be: fruits and milk of cow, boiled only once. For lunch wholemeal flour and boiled vegetables without any condiment except salt, turmeric and a little of cuminseed. A walk at about 5 p.m. and a bath later should be followed by early dinner. He should go to bed at about 9 p.m. with a mud pack on his pubes. The same treatment is equally good for persons suffering from hysteria, menstrual disorders or irregularities and frigidity in women.

(iv) **Impotence**

It is of two types: psychological and organic. Mostly the remedy is psychological, i.e. the patient or the sufferer feels that he is not able to perform the sexual act. Organic impotence related to deficiency in a particular organ for which impotence is symptomatic. In the case of organic impotence, the only way to treat is to deal with the disease which has caused it. The psychological impotence has direct bearing upon some event or tragedy in the past. Then it becomes a disease of nerves and it should be treated accordingly.

Remedy : The general remedy for such a malady is proper diet. Fresh and seasonal fruits and vegetables—raw preferably, germinated grain having lots of vitamins like sprouted moong dal or grams, vigorous physical exercise having an element of competition, adequate sunlight, mud pack on your spine when you retire for the day, sun-bath early in the morning are some of the measures one should take to fight this disorder.

CHAPTER X

SUMMARY TREATMENT CHART

DISEASE	GENERAL PROGRAMME (CP)
For all diseases as specified hereunder (For a required period)	(1) Cold hip bath-evening for 15 minutes followed by brisk walk or Yoga. (2) Mud pack-morning for 15/20 minutes, followed by neem (lukewarm) water enema, if constipated/during fasting. (3) Oil massage for 30/40 minutes (once/twice a week). (4) Sauna/steam bath/sun bath (once/twice a week), if possible. Drink water before any hot treatment. (5) Relaxation, immersion full bath (once/twice a week). (6) Hot Epsom salt bath (twice a week). (7) Fasting on drinking water and juices for a required period. (8) Do *Suryanamaskar*, brisk walk, jogging early morning. (9) Nothing should be eaten 30 minutes before and after any treatment. (10) Do not drink or drink very little water during meal and upto 60 minutes thereafter. (11) Rest, relaxation, sunshine, fresh air, 7 hours sound sleep, vigorous exercises (brisk walk/Yoga) for one hour and strict diet control. (12) Drink one or two glasses of water on rising (early morning). (13) Drink 8/10 glasses (3 litres) of water daily, including lemon, amla,

fruit juices, butter, milk, soups. May take tender coconut water, if suits. (14) Strictly no milk and milk products, frieds, solids, fats, pulses, white rice, banana, potato, maida, sweets, proteins, mango, sapota, salts, ghee, butter and all stimulant/irritant/concentrated food. (15) Avoid smoking, alcohol, zarda, pan-masala, tobacco, drugs, soft drinks, tea, coffee, gas forming food. (16) Eliminate tension, hurry, worry and sedentary habits.

DISEASE	PARTICULAR PROGRAMMES
1. Amoebiasis, constipation, piles.	**GP Plus** GH (Gastro Hepatic) pack, thoroughly cleansing the whole system with fasting and enema for 5 to 10 days, followed by vigorous exercises and controlled diet, hot and cold hip bath and abdominal pack at night. Inject 2/3 millilitres of oil into rectum in the night and put cold pack for 30 minutes on rectum for piles. **Yoga**: Kunjal, Laghushankhaprakshalana, Vipareet Karni, Bhujangasana. Shalabhasana, Dhanurasana, Kapal Bhati, Anuloma Viloma.
2. Indigestion, loss of appetite, gastro intestinal gas.	**GP Plus** GH (Gastro Hepatic) pack, thorough overhauling of the system with fasting and enema for 2 to 5 days, formentation to abdomen, abdomen massage, hot and cold hip bath twice a week, abdomen pack at night. **Yoga**: Kunjal, Pavan Muktasana, Bhujangasana, Shalabhasana, Yogamudra, Anuloma Viloma.
3. Tension, stress, irritability, depression, anxiety sleplessness,	**GP Plus** cold spinal bath twice daily and abdominal pack at night. Avoid acid forming food like starch, protein, fatty items, but take alkaline diet rich in calcium, Vit.

	insomnia	C and B1, plus dairy products (from skimmed milk) and vegetables, fruits, sprouts, naturally sweet curd/butter milk, soyabeans and molasses. Avoid irritants like lemon, sour juices/curds, spices, salt, pickles etc. Take soothing diet.
		Yoga: Jalaneti, Kunjal, Sarvangasana, Matsyasana, Parvatasana, Shavasana, Pranayama and Chittashuddhi.
4.	Liver disorders (hepatitis), amoebic liver	**GP Plus** GH pack, abdominal pack at night, thorough overhauling the whole system with fasting and enema for 6 to 10 days, dry friction, light massage over liver followed by cold and hot fomentation (3 mts. each) or hot and neutral hip bath weekly 2/3 times, hot Epsom salt bath. Take soothing diet.
		Yoga: Kunjal, Halasana, Paschimottanasana, Ustrasana, Shashankasana, Bhastrika, Anuloma Viloma.
5.	Respiratory diseases- asthma, bronchitis, sore throat, cough, allergies, sinusitis, cold, rhinitis, nasal polyps (chornic) nose block.	**GP minus** cold hip bath, plus cold chest pack at night. Fomentation to upper back. Thorough overhauling of the whole system with fasting and enema for 3 to 8 days, dry friction, neutral sponge, breathing exercises, hot Epsom salt bath. Hot water should be sipped when required. Take steam inhalation, asthma bath, back massage, hot arm and hot foot bath (combined for 15 minutes) then sleep immediately at night, rub vicks on chest and throat and cover with woollen muffler before sleeping, keep chest warm by wearing sweater and muffler, do not expose to cold. Gargle with warm salt (saline) water 2/3 times daily. Restricted (mucousless) diet for 3 to 6 weeks. Take fruits and juice rich in Vit.

C. No cooked food in the evenings. Avoid dairy products.

Yoga: Kunjal, Jalaneti followed by cow ghee drop in nostrils, Vastra Dhauti, Laghushankha Prakashalana. Suryanamaskara, Bhujangasana, Shalabhasana, Paschimottanasana, Kapal Bhati, Bhastrika, Suryabhedana and Yoga Nidra.

6. **Migraine, Headache.**   **GP Plus** thorough overhauling of the system with fasting and enema for 3 to 8 days. Hot foot and arm bath, massage to head, contrast foot bath, hot and cold hip bath (twice a week), massage to abdomen, fomentation and pack.

Yoga: Kunjal, Laghu Shankhaprakshalana, Suryanamaskara, Bhujangasana. Shalabhasana, Paschimottanasana, Shitali, Sheetakari, Yoga nidra.

7. **Hypertension (HBP)**   **GP minus** sauna, steam, any hot treatment, jogging, cycling, heavy exercises, Suryanamaskar, Shirshasana, Mayurasana. Take chest/trunk packs, cold spinal bath, ice massage to head and spine, mud bath, hot foot bath with chest pack. Maximum sleep, rest and relaxation (minimum 10 hours daily). Salt is poison. Reverse oil massage weekly twice. Three days on fruit diet every month.

Yoga : Jalaneti, Bhujangasana, Ardha Pavanmuktasana, Parvatasana. Gomukhasana, Sitali, Bhramari, Yoga nidra.

8. **Hypotension (LBP), under-weight, anaemia, fatigue, nervous debility.**   **GP minus** lemon plus sitz bath daily. Drink milk with honey, warm honey water, soups, butter milk, curd, sugarcane juice, boiled vegetables and light nutritious diet. Eat

some fruits, soaked nuts like almonds and roasted grams during day—2-3 times. Increase muscular activity by brisk walk/exercises.

Yoga: Kunjal, Laghushankha Prakshalana, Suryanamaskara, Paschimottanasana, Dhanurasana, Yogamudra, Kapal Bhati, Shirshasana (on apparatus), Bhastrika, Anuloma Viloma.

9. **Diabetes Mellitus**

GP Plus GH pack. Take hot and cold hip bath twice a week and abdominal pack at night. Do more brisk walks and jogging. Take rest, relaxation and sleep for minimum 10 hours daily. Drink *karela* juice, lemon/amla juice, jamun, *mosambi*, vegetable soup, butter milk and curds. To have minimum carbohydrate diet. Reduce working hours. May take some fruits and roasted gram 2-3 times a day.

Yoga: Kunjal, Laghushankha Prakshalana, Suryanamaskara, Dhanurasana, Janusirasana, Ardha Matsyendrasana, Shirshasana. (on apparatus), Kapal Bhati, Bhastrika, Anuloma, Viloma.

10. **Arthritis, rheumatism, spondylitis, back pain, sciatica, lumbago.**

GP minus cold hip bath and cold drinks plus hot Epsom salt bath, fomentation, infra-red to back and pain zones, hot hip bath with salt, hot spinal bath, Kunjal, dry friction. Thorough overhauling of the system with fasting and enema for 6 to 10 days followed by only fruit diet for 10/15 days. Do back bending asanas repeatedly. Use only hard bed, avoid jerks, pillows, long sittings, constipation and citrus fruits. Always have restricted diet-light but nutritious and rich in calcium/Vit. B and D—like skimmed milk and its products are recommended.

Yoga: Jalaneti, Kunjal, Ardha Pavanmuklasana, Katichalana, Uttan Tadasana, Bhujangasana, Parvatasana, Shalabhasana, Dhanurasana, Vakrasana, Kapal Bhati, Anuloma Viloma (simple).

11. Kidney disease

GP Plus kidney pack, drink plenty of water and be only on liquids like juice of wheat grass, cucumber, ashgourd, carrot, lemon, mosambi, orange, cabbage, tender coconut water and dhania water for 3 to 7 days. Strictly no salt, sweets, pluses and milk. Always pass urine immediately after meal.

Yoga: Kunjal, Bhujangasana, Shalabhasana, Vakrasana, Pavan Muktasana. Kapal Bhati, Bhastrika, Anuloma Viloma.

12. Fevers

GP minus cold hip bath, oil massage, any hot treatment and immersion bath. Plus fasting and enema daily, cold chest pack and cold sponges. Total mental and physical rest. Head wash, wet packs on forehead, eyes and abdomen, ice bag on head. Only juices/soup and adequate water intake.

Yoga: Kunjal and Rest.

13. Stomach ulcers, (Gastric and Duodenal)

GP minus any hot treatments, plus abdomen packs at night. Kidney pack. Strictly no exertion, Kunjal, asanas, massage etc., on abdomen. Drink cold diluted cow milk or goat milk with honey. Drink juice of ashgourd, cabbage, carrot, lettuce, orange, fresh butter milk/curd (not sour), use whole flour/brown rice, banana, stewed apple. Avoid all sour fruits, rough vegetables, lemon, guava, pulses, tomato, tamarind, amla, sour curd, spices, chillies and maida.

Yoga: Sitali, Bhramari, Shavasana,

	Yoganidra.
14. Diarrhoea/dysentery colitis.	**GP minus** enema, asana, GH pack, massage plus cold water or butter milk enema once a day and mud pack daily 2 to 4 times, kidney pack. Take butter milk, tender coconut water, honey, ripened banana, baked apple, fresh curd and well cooked rice. Avoid physical exercises, milk, lemon, all other fruits and vegetables. **Yoga**: Rest.
15. Skin diseases.	**GP plus** GH pack, mud bath, neem water bath, dry friction, cold sponge. Epsom salt bath, full wet pack. Only fruit diet for 5 to 10 days intermittently. Avoid sugar, salt, fried food, milk, fats and pulses. **Yoga**: Kunjal (salt free), Suryanamaskara, Dhanurasana, Chakrasana. Paschimottanasana, Shirshasana (on apparatus), Anuloma Viloma.
16. Nausea, hyperacidity, severe hiccups.	**GP Plus** abdomen/trunk packs, ice bag on abdomen and cold spinal bath, take half banana and half glass of chilled milk without sugar 3 hourly, take half galss naturally sweet mosambi or orange juice (cold) 4 hourly. Keep ice cube in the mouth and chew slowly. Must not lose weight. **Yoga**: Bhujangasana, Parvatasana, Gomukhasana, Vakrasana, Sitali, Bhramari.
17. Prostatis— Enlargement of prostate glands (Benign Prostatic Hypertrophy)	**GP Plus** wet girdle pack and ice bag on lower abdomen daily once. Hot or hot and cold alternate hip bath or fomentation to abdomen and abdominal pack weekly 2/3 times. Take soothing diet. Fast one day in a week with juices 4 hourly. Avoid constipation and sexual thoughts. Always take very light and satvik diet.

Yoga: Kunjal, Laghushankha Prakshalana, Pavan Muktasana. Paschimottanasana, Moolabandh, Ashwini Mudra, Anuloma Viloma.

18. Obesity.

GP Plus thorough overhauling of the whole system with fasting and enema for 15 to 30 days followed by soup and only fruit/vegetable diet for several days, vigorous exercise, daily 5 to 10 km brisk walk and full control on palate. Take lemon water 3-5 times daily. Avoid banana, mango, sapota, grapes, potato.

Yoga: Kunjal, Suryanamaskar, Bhujangasana, Shalabhasana, Dhanurasana. Janusirasana, Kapal Bhati, Bhastrika.

19. Menstrual Disorders.

GP Plus abdomen pack every night. Hot and cold hip bath (for painful and scanty menstruation), twice a week to be done throughout the month except during periods. Fomentation to abdomen (if bleeding is not excessive) in case of pain, during periods.

Yoga: Kunjal, Laghushankha Prakashalana, Suryanamaskar, Charkrasana. Dhanurasana, Matsyasana, Garbhasana, Kapal Bhati, Anuloma Viloma.

IMPORTANT : GHP

If the above treatment and diet control seem too much, adopt 50% of them but concerning the disease and suitability—each case has to be assessed individually. Hence obtain advice of a Naturopath and Yoga expert.

Gastro Hepatic Pack (yields excellent results). The Gastro Hepatic Pack influences not only the stomach and liver but also the spleen and pancreas through the intimate association of the circulation of these organs.

DIAMOND POCKET BOOKS PRESENTS
MINI BOOKS

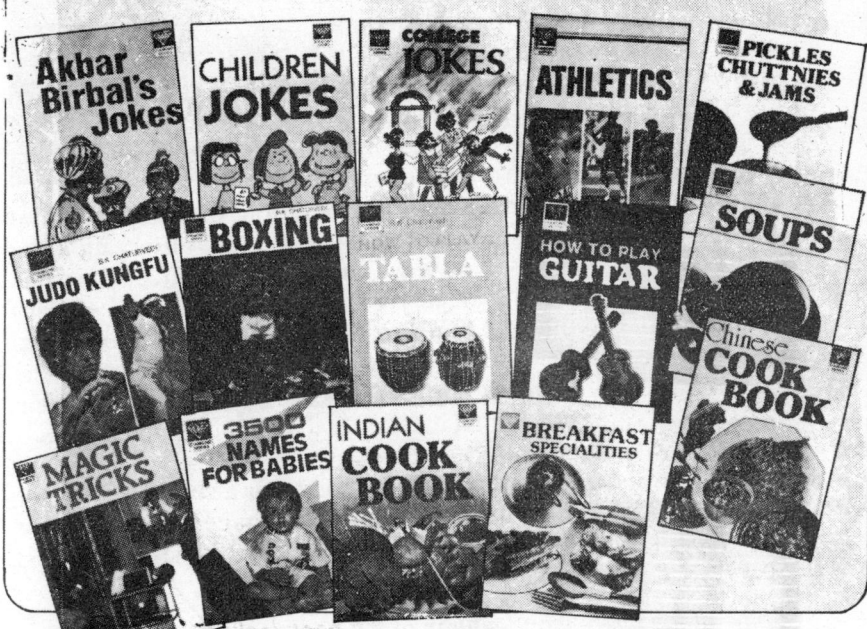

JOKES SERIES				
* Doctor's Jokes	* College Jokes	* Pregnancy & Child Care	* 3500 Names for Babies
* Mad Jokes	* Lawyer's Jokes	* All about Female Sexual Disorder	* Efficient House Keeping
* Hot Jokes	* Engineer Jokes	* Sex for young Couples	* Numerology
* Latest Jokes	* Political jokes	* Enhance Your Sexual Potency	* Face Reading
* Funny Jokes	**GAMES SERIES**	* 101 Questions about Sex & Their Answers	* Develope Your Personality
* Great Jokes	* How to Play Volley Ball	* Sex for Adolescens	* Public Speaking
* Jokes for All	* Athletics	**MUSIC SERIES**	* Basic Computer Knowledge
* Jokes, Jokes & Jokes	* Swimming	* How to Play Tabla	* Diamond Guide to Palmistry
* Filmi Jokes	* Judo Kungfu	* How to Play Harmonium	* Astrology
* Top Jokes	* Judo Karate	* How to Play Guitar	**COOKERY SERIES**
* Akbar Birbal Jokes	* Boxing	* How to Play Flute	* Fruit Drinks & Cordials
* Professional Jokes	* Gymnastic	* How to Play Sitar	* Indian Cook Book
* Party Jokes	* How to Play Cricket	**OTHER SERIES**	* Breakfast Specialities
* Midnight Jokes	* How to Play Hockey	* Kitchen Gardening	* Bengali & Other Sweets
* Selected Jokes	* How to Play Football	* Magic tricks	* Mughlai Cook Book
* Modern Jokes	* How to Play Tennis	* Be An efficient Secretary	* South Indian Cook Book
* Children Jokes	* How to Play Badminton	* How to improve your English	* Pickle Chuttnies & Jams
* Lover's Jokes	* How to Play Table Tennis	* How to Succeed in	* Gujarati Cook Book
* Tenalirama Jokes	**SEX SERIES**	* Share Market	* Soups
* Office Jokes	* Body Care During & After Pregnancy	* Some Tried & Tated Domestic Formula For Money Saving	* Ice Cream Cakes & Pasteries
	* Breast Care	* How to Become a Millionaire	* Chinese Cook Book
	* Family Planning & Birth Control		* Punjabi Cook Book
			* Vegetarian Cook Book
			* Non Vegetarian Cook Book

PUBLISHED BY : **DIAMOND POCKET BOOKS (P) LTD.** X-30, OKHLA INDUSTRIAL AREA PHASE-II, NEW DELHI-110020

A Mantra to Develop Brain

Biswaroop Roy Chowdhury, an authority in brain and learning techniques and National Memory Record holder, combines ancient wisdom and latest scientific Key Techniques of Memory (KTM), as a way to memory development. In his book **'Dynamic Memory Methods'**, the young Memory Consultant has given tips regarding the use of scientific memory techniques for memorising faster and retaining it longer.

Based on mnemonics (artificial aids to learning) and laws of controlled association, the simple mental exercises mentioned in the book enhances reader's observation and concentration in an amazing way. The regular practice of various techniques mentioned inculcates the habit of using creative (Right) part of brain and thus the brain's capacity is optimized owing to balanced use of both logical (Left) and creative part of the brain. The book teaches 100 memory codes of memory language which help the reader in developing mental catalogue so that they can make their recalling and remembering effective.

The book is useful for all, a business person or a student, young or old; as familiarity with the memory language also helps in remembering telephone numbers, vocabulary, names and faces, speeches and anecdotes more efficiently.

Some of the interesting features of the book include:

- Making learning a fun
- Advanced Mnemonic System
- Curing absent-mindedness.
- Increase in intellect and positive mental attitude
- How to study smarter and not harder
- Preparing for competitive exams
- Remembering long answers of history.
- Memorising geographical maps & biological diagrams

RECEIVE BOOKS AT HOME BY VPP POSTAGE Rs. 10.00 (Extra)
ON ORDER OF THREE OR MORE BOOKS POSTAGE FREE

DIAMOND POCKET BOOKS
X-30, Okhla Industrial Area, Phase-II, New Delhi - 110 020
Phone No. : 011-6841033, 6822803, Fax : 011-6925020

'डाइनैमिक मेमोरी मेथड्स' हिन्दी एवं बंगाली में भी उपलब्ध है। प्रत्येक का मूल्य 60.00